AVENGING CARTOGRAPHY

KEN POYNER

Barking Moose Press, LLC
www.barkingmoosepress.com

AVENGING CARTOGRAPHY

Ken Poyner

Grateful acknowledgement is made to the following publications in which some of these pieces previously appeared:

Artificial Selection Project: Cosmetic Dentistry

Black Denim: Establishment; Snake Oil Rights

Blackwire: Evolution

Blue Fifth: Cocking the Fulcrum; Yugoslavia

Broadkill Review: Manufacture

Café Irreal: Suspicion

Corium: Joy in the Sense of Place; Reasonable

Cream City Review: The Love House

Crooked Shift: Diminishing Returns

Danse Macabre: The Lightning Gatherers; The Daughter Comes of Age; Contraband; The Craftsman

decomP: The Bear Seeks a Position in Accounting

Emprise Review: The First Meal

Every Day Fiction: Justice

Farther Stars Than These: A Change of Address

Fleeting: The Confusion

Full of Crow: The Culinary Advance; The Science of Books

Garbanzo: Suburbia

Gone Lawn: The Abduction

Hidden Animals: Commerce

Journal of Microliterature: The Reason; The Selfishness of Work; Our Monkeys; The Artist

Lime Hawk: The Encounter

Linguistic Erosion: Relative Economics

Literary Orphans: Courting

Manic Fervor: The Value of Schedule

Menda City: Connection

Table of Contents

INTRODUCTIONS

"Honey, the house is moving!" my wife says. She has always been direct.

"No, it is not." I mutter from beneath one of four or five blankets and cats. My warmth is not something I give up easily.

"Wake up!" she says like a sneeze, "Yes, it is."

I lie still for a moment and just barely I can feel something. Not falling, nor rising. Not shaking.

I think for a moment this is one of those dreams where you sit up in bed and the bed is afloat on an azure sea, calm enough that you have slept far out away from shore, and all that slides around you is still water.

I get up by carefully easing myself out of bed like a knife from a sheath. At the window I peer out of the crack in the curtain that appears every night, and just in time see the corner streetlight pass behind us.

I look at my wife and say, "The house is moving!" She is out of bed before the arc of bed sheets settles back to the mattress. Single file down the stairs we run and open incautiously the front wooden door (knowing of course the glass and metal security door would protect us).

Before we are oriented, she breathes over my shoulder, "Look, 813 is moving, too." And it is. Edging along on its foundation-remains like a stiff sidewinding rattler, it is moving along the street into the open space vacated by the house beside it—which is moving, too. We do not know the occupants of 813, even though they have lived across from us for a decade, but one has breeched a second floor window and is hanging out, trying to look up the street to where our houses are going.

A few of our neighbors stand still in the street having escaped their homes, and we quickly pass them: dim, unknown others who have lived around us for a year or fifteen, now behind us and gone.

My wife, her fingers now in my shoulder, says, "Should we jump? Should we? From the stoop we would clear the track all the houses are making, we could double back to where the neighbors are."

I say, "But we don't really know them. I haven't waved to one of them in years." By now we have gone perhaps a hundred yards from the slab that for twenty-three years has supported us and the house. I worry the floor tile will break up. A dog I do not recognize is barking and from spots of darkness a baby here or there is beginning the locomotive of a good cry.

I unlatch the security door's thumb latch, wrap both arms about the wife, and make one huge backward lunge and in seconds we are free, free and watching our house snake its way with so many others deep into the rustling brick and lumber of the city.

As we walk back to where our house had been and where our small lick of land still is, someone loosely familiar catches up with us and asks, "Do you know what this is about?" and I introduce myself.

THE TABLEAU

The falls are beautiful this time of year. They have a quickness to them; a full-throated brevity lashed between points of sullen gravity; the nonchalant character of a summation. We can ingest them all in one staggering horizon's breadth, cause and effect seen as one line, forced into one round. A clattering instant of electric discharge. It takes no effort to understand them. Neither winds nor cold, nor even a seldom rain, intervenes. The weather in this season complements our mission. Each fall is pure, crystalline.

Carefully we rate every one we capture. That woman's trip was but a two: she stumbled, pitched a half step forward, caught herself, and continued without even searching for the interruption. The man half an hour ago was a seven: he took two quick hops, lilted to one knee, pulled himself around to see where his foot had faulted, to hopefully discern what environmental leprechaun had felled him.

We converse on the proper score. Archetypes from past experience are recalled and mental comparisons made. Unless everyone agrees to the score, there can be no standard. Given the infinite ways in which a fall can be accomplished, our deliberations can be contentious. Feelings are hurt. Tendencies understood. One of us might value falling backward more than falling forward. Another might have a fondness for windmill arms, or landings with legs out vice landings with legs curled. Each element lends its peculiarity to the whole. It is important to respect all inputs, to consider the unlikely as well as the obvious. The fall may be judged as a unit, but it has oh so many fingers and toes and each has its own voice.

Once a man went sideways to keep from going flat out and, with this ungainly maneuver, in the end broke his underdeveloped leg. It was the first serious injury to befall us in our occupation. He was taken off by an ambulance, gasping at every bump when the gurney was hoisted into the back. After that we left off rating the falls for several days. We stopped hoping ordinary people would catch and collapse. We became citizens less of observation and more of noble intention. But in the end, we realized that, rated or not, the falls would occur. People—observed or not, counted or not, graded or not—would go down. No matter how we apprehended the physical manifestation, the underlying events would stagger cold-bloodedly on. People would fall. Injuries would be no gosling pleasure for anyone, but the fact of our artistic appreciation, of our ranking the aesthetics to be wrung out of the occurrence, would itself damage no one.

And this was that special time of year, when those who fell would be wearing their summer attire, often in shorts or shirt sleeves: some even sleeveless, with elbows and forearms likely to suffer abrasion if, as with the best of the falls, the stubbed actually were to go all the way down, splay out like a cephalopod dropped from a cooler onto the pavement. In this season, no fall can be blamed on coat tails or trailing scarves; no mere hitch in locomotion can be hidden in layers of outer garments. Every misstep is cinematic: the writhing of the muscles as they attempt to compensate can be with an open line of sight enjoyed; the aerodynamics of collapse can be tasted.

Imagine the falls we have seen. All those thuds and thumps that most people would let pass unnoticed. And consider the joy we feel when, ourselves pinned unaware, we stumble and pitch forward or back, falling, falling, momentarily unable to crack gravity in the shin: wholly without a break to the physics of the matter, taken out of ourselves and given over to mass and common attraction. Our joy. And every one of our own electrifying falls is a ten.

One unknowing performer once said: someone is going to break their neck one day. And we knew it to be true. Someone will: someone ungainly, inelegant, too slow to right himself. Maybe someone unmanageably careless in attention: focused on the task ahead, the approaching end rather than the current means. Or simply someone strapped by his or her own hubris to a developing series of events: a series that ends with a broken neck. And when it occurs, it should be at this time of year, on a day as glass-edged as this one: the fall a clear geometry of fallow flailing, the gravity washed body deserving, the fall so righteous as to independently glow. That fall would be a ten, and we would feel the proud physics of it in our stomachs as though it were ourselves falling: surrendering; reliving every fall we had ever seen; loving with near sexual verve that final crack of exposition, that snap of affirmation.

THE VALUE OF SEA URCHIN
HEART ICE CREAM

When they drove up and climbed out of the tank, the wife watched undaunted from the front window, bent sensually over the couch like a girl in a cheap hotel expecting quick work, and trying not to be spotted at the barely parted curtains. She had never seen a live merman. All she knew of mermen was what she had read in the tabloids, picked up from comic books, or had lazily watched late night on the natural history channel when nothing desperate was on elsewhere. Add what she had heard as rumors and fears and prejudices and wishes.

We could not pronounce their names. We do not have the necessary organs.

Pleasantries went quickly. It was obvious they had come to eat. From first wallowing in at the front door, they had their eyes fixed on the dining room table. They declined to sit in the living room chairs, conveniently explaining that they did not want to stain the furniture, and that their tails were much more manageable in something hard-backed and flat. Their eyes darted always to the table, and I think they made great show that dry gravity was an imposition for them, their hunger a compensation.

In our house, you can see through from the foyer to the dining room and on to the pass-through with the kitchen. I never wondered, before then, whether that design could be disadvantageous. In one unadulterated view you have a man's downstairs life accounted for.

We had hardly sat down to the table before they began ferociously on the shrimp. Bare handed. The wife and I struggled with our utensils while they pulled and sucked and consumed some items gloriously whole. Their long fingers worked as though they were playing multi-stringed instruments, and their elbows flared warlike and recklessly. The shrimp tussled and cracked and popped and snaked and inedible pieces fell where unbuoyed gravity called them. My wife excused herself and brought back a large bowl to hold the leavings: what few leavings there were, what fewer there might be.

The talk was of shrimp: river mouth shrimp versus ocean shrimp versus gulf shrimp versus varieties of shrimp we land creatures do not yet have names for. And there were some references to crawfish. Size and texture and how to lie in wait for shrimp, how to call them by their uncommon names during wrinkles in the filtering moonlight at the indulgence of the shallows.

I knew early on that this had been a bad idea. There are some species that are simply incompatible, no matter how personable individual members might be. You imagine what conspiratorial collaboration could evolve, you see the mental picture of brotherhood, of being linked if not yoked to common goals; but the physics and chemistry do not exist to get you there. Science crosses its legs, looks you in the eye, and tells you that you are an idiot. But you wish it were different, and you wish simply for the nobility of wishing it were different. And science, after all, is a recent invention.

I saw in my wife's face that she was meeting her tolerances. The color seemed to waffle along her cheeks, and her spine was bent far too aggressively, her feet flat and together at the heels. She could, at times like these, form herself into a pencil, command the world to be her paper. The shrimp shredded, the lull lasting no time at all, the merman teetering nearest the wife reached across the table to grab whole one of the drearily reddened lobsters. He bent awash against our table in full ownership, drafted with the anticipation of the other mermen, the expectation of gain. It was then my wife leaned forward, and, as best she could with her thin and angular features, made what she surely imagined was the best, most dryly outlandish fish face she could net. Pursed lips, eyes wide, cheeks sunken, the sound of bubbles laced in her outgoing breath.

I braced. The mermen stopped in their assault on our table and its exhausting spread. The wife leaned even more forward, rising inches from her chair, her supporting arms ribbons of intent, pushing her faux fish face out over the littered and silent table. I was quickly thinking survival, running through equations of conviviality: I can make this a joke, I was thinking; I can push this desperation into humor, into slapstick, into a story of family history.

The mermen put down their food. They settled back in their chairs, more cautious with their frictions and weight than ever before this. And they smiled. They smiled, showing the jagged tips of their front rows of teeth, and flared their gills and cocked their heads and their tails whipped forward, riling and dimpling the well-worn carpet.

My wife leaned ever recklessly more forward and began to pulse her lips, to work her shoulders, to sculpt her back: and the mermen smiled with their eyes, with the curve of their water weary bodies. Their scales shimmered a bit at their waists and the stalks just over their ears went fully, gleefully erect. One began, low in his throat, to teasingly vibrate: the leathery skin rolling across the glimmering recessed organs of his self-expression.

When what seemed like the eldest merman slipped to the edge of his chair and asked my wife if she would like to see their tank, I thought: I had merely gone fishing; I had been bored with the lack of a catch; I had conversed casually of fish habits, pier pylons, where in depth the most desirable fish imbibe. I was the good neighbor. I had done my part for species understanding and mutual discovery. Had I done too much? Were we two masters of our domains simply too different?

But when my wife pushed back her chair and said yes, I felt that rudder of burden lift. And, as the four of them slithered ever so seductively out of the front door, no doubt to brine and froth in the subdued tank parked under wide public scrutiny in my driveway, I thought at least the ice cream with sea urchin hearts we had saved for last would be all mine.

THE CHILDREN OF PASSIVITY

It is the wife's job to replenish the monsters in the closet. Her balance is better than mine.

They get out at night and go roaming asunder like underclothes in a tornado. Mornings when we cannot get them all back in I am off running through the neighborhood in my shorts, looking for closet monsters, or even the leavings of monsters. You can track them by their scat. Or by the warmth they leave in morning air, like the impression an old-fashioned fire place iron leaves in modern cloth.

I can occasionally round up one, seldom two, and the others are gone: superseded, vaporized in the early air of practicality and the silly science of ordinary sustenance.

And so the wife replenishes them. It does not matter the manner of monster. She stuffs the closet with any generic monster she can find: monsters escaped from other couples' closets, itinerant monsters, monsters temporarily down on their luck, monsters caught unaware. She knows our tenuous humanity is the sum of our emotional fears. I think that is why I married her.

It is true, about our emotional fears. Look it up if you fail to believe me.

All day the closet monsters stay in place, playing cards or cribbage or listening to pornography on the small radio we let them keep. They gamble, tossing dice against the back wall where our dress shoes usually mingle and mate, cherishing their privacy. It is not a bad closet during the day. The door seals out all but a tinkering of light at the floor sweep, just a hint of contamination.

They know the drill. The wife and I drift into bed and, after any hair pin lustful gymnastics, pull the sheets up under our chins. We look like potatoes in aluminum foil, ready for the straggling coals that have already shot their best into the seduction of the main course. Our eyes are as wide as the headlights of container trucks: spots of reference that can both reveal and blind.

And then the tapping from the inside of the closet door begins. At first an occasional rap: and then an effervescent execution of mixed patterns, as constant as a point between two idle lines.

Usually, the wife fetches the first glass of water. Soon after, I get the second. And later it is a story, an overly drawn tale of when monsters were not relegated to the closet but had their own kingdoms and ate the bones of rivals, and trawled the night for Darwin's rejected victims, and made blue smoke whenever they wanted to.

When stories end, even I am surprised these lustful shells can be tamed with a snack of pretzel sticks, or sour-cream-and-onion potato chips.

We do our best to be efficient keepers of monsters confined; yet, invariably, one or more slips out of the closet: distracted, one of us leaves the door ajar; or they wait for us to turn the ever glittery knob, and then as many of them flash through at the first crack of light as can crowd into line. There is no need to search for them in the over filled night. For all their mainstream ineffectiveness, being part of the night is what they are bred for, what still remains intact of their sad realms. They blend in like flies in a herd of geese migrating west: you see and hear the geese, you note that they are headed west, but you would not pick out a hitchhiking fly.

I don't know why they want out. All of us—including the complete, emasculated tangle of them—feel better in possession of a closet full of diminished monsters. Any escape lessens us. If we cannot drag them back, the monsters themselves end up living under the Sixth Street bridge: trying to frighten bums out of a secondhand bag of fries; or spinning dark gravity behind a mother with a grocery sack, hoping for edible spillage. Now and then they apply at the relief organization and you might see a closet monster raking leaves, for not much more than the price of a lunch, outside of the girls' winsome dorm at City College. I take them back when I can find them. I let the wife make them a good offer. We get them again to be sterile and happy, if only for just a while.

Don't think it our charity. We at least have monsters in our closet, even if they are undeserving, boring, and taken to ambling off into the night. How many people have no monsters at all? They sleep secure in their beds, the pathetic evenness of their dreams as expected as waking the next morning, as expected as sleeping soundly the next night, as expected as the calculus of their mutually unremembered sex. Who could want that? At least for us there is hope that one day we will have a monster in the closet whose smile is just a bit more than bare testament to his mediocre disutility: that one day his escaping the closet will be no escape at all, but a method of relevance. Living in the possibility of that day makes this drudgery against ungrateful closet monsters worth every sleep-abandoned minute of it, worth the investment of our effortlessly rare hope.

COCKING THE FULCRUM

There was a boy on the sidewalk today who had one of those "Hungry, please help" signs, so, as I went by, I gave him a quick sweep to the shin and gloriously like broken wind chimes down he went. He did not even drop his sign: but he did have to carefully put it aside to set himself back up.

There is so much violence in the world. All the media are obsessed with conflict programming. Everything is so whirligig loud. Everything is opposition ego, stratification rite. It becomes important to let one's own aimless violence out, to clear the evolving static from the skull, to make a temporary peace with one's inner needs. It must be done: what is important is how you do it.

You can't take your soup of boiled anger to bed. You can't commit your sedative of replacement violence against a peer or superior: that just would not work. More conflict. More competition. No. You have to strike down, downward, decently low: to those beneath the concern line.

I felt so much better when that boy went over. I could carelessly sip a full breath directly between my currently stylish lips. The air tasted like the engaged sexuality of unrecognized children. It was like the flush of pure blue advocate electrons being set perilously free behind the bridge of my nose. For a full half an hour I did not think that I needed a new car, or was cramped in my home, or needed to worry about the worth of erections.

My wife takes a less purist approach. She would have loudly lectured everyone on the corner, as though they were fish glued with a living epoxy to the side glass of an aquarium, about how poor children should be in orphanages, and put to learning trades: be given the permanent satisfaction of a career in service and manual labor. These children could start with yard work now, she would tell them; then they might end up profitably clearing drainage ditches; and they could, perhaps, one day, bespeckled with coveralls and a utilitarian second hand hat, grow into running machinery, or measuring macadam with whimsically blue chalk lines that automatically retract.

For a mercurially usable time afterwards she might be less randomly combative, more cream scented sure of herself, more giving of her unaccounted-for time: ready to let a peer be a peer. After unexpectedly meeting, diligently recharged, in the hall, we might lazily lumber through a curious foreplay, and execute our marriage without the salt-tasting, dagger-tipped haze usually winding in our self-gratifying fluids, that worries of who in this episode might be getting mechanically the better of whom.

Maybe I should shepherd her down to that corner.

REASONABLE

They are not so rare as they once were. Ordinary people have seen them: practical picnickers gone a bit away from the group, tossing their tablecloths off the path beyond gravel and mechanically mown grass; hikers; children seeking a natural privacy for tuning their understandings of sex. These commercial beasts have become practically ubiquitous.

At one time, you only saw them as metal or plastic caricatures, mounted with steel beams and wires outside of chicken palaces, each more brazenly advertising the best chicken sandwich on the planet, demanding that all the other places raise their own unrealistically huge chicken effigies. I've seen them painted blue. One chicken sandwich is much like all the other chicken sandwiches, but the faux giant chickens hoisted in hyperbole would vary in presentation as much as an isolated small businessman's mind could reach.

Back then, real eight or nine foot chickens were as rare as hen's teeth. It took a tracker, and a team of four or five, to ferret one out, run him around half a day until his exhaustion would allow us to slip up and with team effort wring his python-like neck.

They are so common nowadays, I expect to be reading about giant chickens being killed in automobile accidents, shot by citizens who find them nosing about in the trash on their patios. An industry will spring up for collecting the stray accidental kills, processing them into chicken sandwiches, assuring the driver or homeowner that nothing is going to waste. There will be signs showing how the cost of a dented fender can be reduced with the bounty from a chicken kill and a cut on all the sandwich slabs salvageable.

Mark my words: men like me will become rarer and rarer; and, one day, there will be no need for us at all.

Still, though, focused on the present, we make a good living tracking the gargantuan fowl. Once you find one, then you and your team have got to bring him down. The claws at the end of those perilous three toes can rip the innards of a man completely out with only a glancing blow. You worry about the beak, expecting him to nip your head off or pry though your chest and eat the heart—only to have the feet whip around and slit you into three definable pieces. You stay on the balls of your feet. You look for the sway of the coxcomb to warn you of a change in movement. You feel the breath of the feathers.

We have lost people. Handlers have come back with fewer appendages than they went out with. But just one nine foot chicken dropped can be processed into enough chicken sandwiches to make a man, even the most junior handler, six months of ordinary wages. A processing plant can get more chicken sandwiches out of one of our feral giant chickens than they can with a full load of standard flock chickens. There is less waste, more percentage sandwich meat. With these, the inedible parts get more readily separated out. The byproducts are more manageable. They are proof of the economy of scale.

In my career, I've been responsible for at least a quarter million sandwiches; I have been the proud engine for feeding thousands with high quality gargantuan chicken meat, pressed and re-hydrated: situated between two white buns, and with any variety of condiments. I think, even under lettuce and onion and sweet sauce, I can tell the wild, tracker provided giant chicken meat from the farmer's flock of small, yard reared fowl. I look forward to coming back from an expedition and claiming that first chicken sandwich, the sensation of unwrapping it and tossing the paper into the landfill bin: that steam coming off of the fresh meat, and the subtle twang to the taste, that tells me this chicken had been run to ground, hand wrung, pulled back out of the deep woods by men who know the cost of a meal.

Once I worked with a handler who used to talk about chicken legs and chicken wings and chicken breasts. He would opine how just one leg from one of these humongous chickens, grilled, could feed a family of six for a week; and how one breast could last through a summer church social. He would share the size by spreading his hands, use the distance between trees to demonstrate how large he would imagine the entrée might be. He could talk of open fire pits, the mechanics of suspending unprocessed meat, filets you would have to assault with a knife and fork. Sandwiches were not in his veins. He lasted less than one season.

I hope that even deep into the woods, now that eight and nine foot tall gigantic chickens are showing up way too commonly in the very suburbs, there might be twelve or thirteen foot chickens. Chickens we have never gotten to because we were too infatuated with the smaller giants just into the border dark of the lolling unknown. Fowl that could spy on you in your second floor apartment, whose meat could make a processing plant smoke and whirl into the night, providing the blue suited workers welcomed overtime.

If we can find such suspected larger prey, imagine how many sandwiches each would produce, how many buns and the vats of condiments that would be consumed. These fowl could be more dangerous, the tracking more hideously involved, the handlers greater in numbers and more likely to demand higher shares. The plants would run night and day and the sandwiches stack up in mounds beneath the heat lamps. All those cotton-dry sandwiches! Thousands lying in their warming shelves as we count our bounties and the public stands in line clamoring for more! Pressed meat: with our tracking crews remaining the champions of the hunt, the fearless providers of the feast. A special set of men unwilling to accept the utility of the house flock; men who seek the wild to feed into the grinder; men who still go out into the dark to bring home our processed food foundation.

Little children would bite down feathered in awe.

A CHANGE OF ADDRESS

I have wanted to sell my slot on the station's planet side for some time. I'm tired of the payments. I'm tired of the taxes. I'm tired of the zoning ordinances.

I can rent a half-day berth on the interior, let some landlord worry about all the minutia of property ownership. I work a full twelve hours each day, so I can split a place with someone who works an opposite shift. We might pass in the hallway.

The problem is that the Nanurian three doors down holds my mortgage. I can't sell the place without satisfying that mortgage. I took it out with the station credit bank as a standard payments-over-time instrument three years ago. It got set free on the commodities market, was picked up by a consortium of investment miners, then ended up on the table in a card game on the Pluto 9 station. I think the Nanurian took it for services rendered one week in route on a battered ore liner, limping with a lonely crew into the asteroid belt ore processor plants to off-load.

But it does not matter. She has my mortgage and if I want to sell, I have to settle it.

But it gets more complicated. Seems she has taken out insurance on the full term return on the loan and counter balanced it with insurance on the early pay off penalties. Then she securitized those and sold the whole bundle as an investment product to a consortium who broke it, with others, into shares and now part of my promise to pay is owned by a Eudorian on the other side of the galaxy whose primary business is owning a Fiztick brothel tucked into the interdimensional shift between two gravity reclamation projects.

Ownership of my eight by twelve by six home, with a prime forty-two square inch window on the planet below, is stretched across thirty habitable systems; in the portfolios of eighteen governments, four welfare societies and thirty-one investment unions; and who knows how many private profit greed-warrior clans. The problem now is back value: the worth of the property is in part set by the expectation of returns on the investment quality of the insurance on the investment risk in the insurance bundles on the securitized underlying insurance contract on the investment return discounted by the risk of under-performance on the projected returns, minus prepayment guarantees, on the property itself.

So, if I tell the Nanurian that I want to satisfy my mortgage, she is going to contact all those investment brokers, who are going to contact all the major index agents, and, instantly, what I can get for my slot is going to fall: both as an aggressive market reaction to investment profit risk, and as an actual redistributed risk value against the proposed following market offering of the new owner's mortgage.

So, I came up with the plan.

I take out rental income insurance on the property, basing the face value of the insurance innocuously on the going rates in this quadrant, for a home on this type of station, with a prime slot, planet side. I sell the insurance to the Nanurian, who flashes red and orange with the idea of being doubly indemnified, and hopefully offers me one of the free ports she has open on Thursday now with the shipping out of the Fallorian concessions manager who paid her good money for her thoughtfully divided attentions. Either way, the Nanurian then gets one of her regular customers to buy an option on the insurance, betting the return against risk is going to go down and thus drop the investment value. He then sells the potential difference in value to an investment firm that takes its own insurance against the projected margin, and sells that insurance to a mining company in one of the unnamed asteroid belts around one of the unnamed suns stuck in an unpopulated galactic arm. That mining company uses the financial instrument as paper collateral on a straight cash loan to buy face value stock in an atmosphere manufacturing company that holds a four percent interest in a mining equipment company, hedging that investment with an interest in transmutation technologies, insuring the risk with a grounding in insurance stocks against mortgage payment profits that themselves are backed by a percentage lien on the underlying insured mortgage properties.

When the actual recall value of the mortgage itself gets below one percent of the profit stream in the products securing the mortgage, I set myself up in the market to sell short by missing one mortgage payment, and watch the interdependencies fall back on one another like the million-offspring march of the Proximus Thule elongated fractal frace.

So, I rent, on paper, to a Thelurian miner, who would not fit into the place even during his thin cycle, for a pile of cash, a six-eyed wink, and a purely innocent belief on his part that somewhere in the stream he is going to share in the profits.

And then I knock on the Nanurian's door next Thursday, with a bottle of Tellurian champagne, a lace crusted safety tether, and a change of address.

SUBURBIA

So, I am not much to look at, but I am sturdy. Pretty isn't of much use if it is fragile. Unless your aim is to break it. Breaking pretty is an entirely different passion than the one I live for, and far less practical. You can only break pretty once, then you have to go out and get more pretty, and then you break that pretty, and then you go out for more and the cycle starts all over again. Hard to develop a relationship that way. Hard to lay out your future and survive the mortgage.

I am broad and serviceable. I can take a lot of wear. I can keep coming back for more. Just when anyone thinks I am all figured out, I add an addition, spin for new curtains, put a safety screen on the back French doors. As fickle as an untrained cat, I might add stepping stones in the front garden, or grow a new hedge. I might have a tree surgeon in for that stick that has persisted in my side yard for years. I can be rough on any one unprepared. My guttering has that worldly look, and I've been through a hail storm or two.

I'm not always the best of mates. I've spat out a family or two. I've sat empty, my best makeup on and showing a bit more through my glass than the neighbors think proper. Keep me vacant long enough, and I start getting that hey-sailor lean and bit of an easy glide to the angles of my roof. The ranch across the street begins to rankle in disapproval and the split level beside starts nattering to the two-story brick home next to her and shrugging a cold cornice at me. The whole block goes atwitter at the possibility that I will take up with short term tenants, toy a few months with some unkempt immigrant crew, become a home base for a rowdy collection of bachelors that have nothing better to do than slam my doors and crack my windows and run their smoke-stained fingers along my buttery siding.

I take what I can get. Everyone wants a nuclear family: two adults, two kids, a dog and a cat; maybe the step-son on weekends. The good ones like that are already taken. There were few of them to begin with. You end up with the single parent and six kids, or three girls sharing expenses with an encyclopedia of boyfriends. Even if you think your tenants are going to turn out with the perfect profile, you find that they are wall markers or put nails in the backs of interior doors or want to take out your carpet and put in laminate.

I've seen my share of abuse. My hot water heater has busted. I've had feral moisture down my non-load bearing walls and I have lost shingles for seemingly no reason. I have had the most hideous security door available in America plastered right across my face while I tried to shy-back protectively from the street. I've had basketballs eager to dent my garage door set loose in sky-threatening flocks. I've had holes dug into my underground pipes and I've had muck no one should have to smell spread lazily across my yard and then tracked into the kitchen.

You could do less well than being stuck with me. I might not steam of sex and convenience, but I can shimmer with service and support. And when you are stuck paying the upkeep, what really do you want?

I keep coming back. Year after year, when the less substantial wisps that have lured them away grow spindly and worn, the disenchanted tenants come back to me and I am again their centering agent. I may not be the house they want to go to bed with, but I am the house they want to wake up with. I can carry on a conversation in the morning. I can meet the parents. I can look serviceable in a housecoat and fuzzy slippers. People, this isn't a honeymoon, it's a life. When you are done with that architectural floozy you inhabit now; the one that at original sale vapidly met your immediate, sophomoric and unspeakable needs; meeting them to the point where you were happily out of breath and wondering just what else needed upkeep and attention: welcome that feeling of warming-want you will get when you drive by and in front of my supporting curves and solidly sensuous angles there is that wickedly understated FOR SALE sign, and electrically you can feel the tap tap tapping growth of a desire that can crawl mechanically into bed every night, slide stallion-like onto its side, and ask, always again, if the tangle of the front door might be unlocked.

THE CONTENTION
OF THE LIGHTNING

I carried the lightning gingerly out of the backyard, grasping it with one hand, but cradling it with the other. I had been sitting in my boxer-briefs and hoping one of the cats would break into song when I heard the bolt come crashing through the no-account runt of a holly tree out back, a contagion of disassembled noises that nearly knocked me out of my deep cushioned chair. I stumbled upstairs, looking out of the haplessly cluttered back bedroom window, and I could see it lying there: all its feral electricity drained, or never amassed, the body of it appearing like a cardboard cut out of deflated potential. It looked like it might have hit the tree, glanced, knocked the wind out of itself, then decided to spend its last identifiable moments gasping flat in my yard.

I put on my shorts, socks, and a T-shirt from the not expensive stack, and the shoes I've been thinking I should reserve for cutting the yard. The clumsily gathering storm had not yet begun and yet it had seemed to have shut its mouth already.

I went out the back door.

I am no expert on lightning, but to me this bolt looked surely dead. I don't know what I expected, but it was as light as a child's dance recital when I warily picked it up. I put it back down immediately, having expected a whole lot more. But it did have a cat-like metal feel to it, as though unbalanced electricity might have run dance-hall drunk through it: that it could have had a voice like the batteries of salt, like closet monsters set loose into the day's primping sun.

I unlocked the back gate and kicked it formally open past the grass grown up that always tries to hold it still like a lover only half-way to consent. The key back in my pocket, I picked that lightning up and balanced it on my right shoulder so easily my left hand had nothing to do. Oh, it was not long or unwieldy. It had a smooth gait, a lick-in-the-air-like pacing, a balance that almost seemed to shift to any point you wanted to be its center. Eventually, impressed with the gravity of my conquest, I switched around to one hand on the point, one hand on the shaft, the lightning in front of me like a presentment.

You see, I was simply going to carry it out into the front yard and stand it by the fence where, on Wednesdays, the trash truck comes seeking odd items. After all, the holly tree was none the worse for collision, the grass was barely dented, and I was almost dressed. It was time to deal with the status of the lightning. I am usually not one to procrastinate, and lightning mid-trash week is no different from lightning that strikes on trash day alone. It all looks the same from a distance.

But when I got to my side yard, out front the neighbors, in various states of undress and silly dress and preparedness, were standing in the street behind my driveway: their faces stuck slightly forward at the edges of their tilted heads, their yellow teeth withdrawn. Apparently, they had heard the ungainly calamitous fall better than I, had traced the event to my house or to the reckless common between. There must have been seven of them, with two more coming from further back in our neighborly circle.

I stopped when I saw them. I thought about my T-shirt and shoes. I thought about whether my shorts were long enough to cover the legs of my boxer-briefs. I was prepared to surrender the lightning. My mind was beginning to form around a blue spark of explanation, though I had no idea, then or now, why I would need even a poor explanation. And then, one of the newer residents began to applaud, slamming her palms together all by herself, as though knocking the dust out of a rented carpet, pounding out a rhythm for probably ten seconds or so. And then the others mechanically joined in. Seals at an aquarium show. There, in the semi-dark they stood irregularly clustered, making the sounds of an audience. I love my neighbors, or the spectacles they make of themselves.

And I set that lightning bolt down right there like so many kettles of fish. I walked out to them, to hand shakes and arm slaps, and one portentous slap on the bum, and I led them into my side yard to let them see the lightning directly, to stroke the cold skin of it: but not lift it, not claim its heft. I told them of its courageous electricity, the fierceness of its grasp, the deep aquamarine thunder none of them had heard, and the struggle beside the holly tree. I was an alien before the second retelling.

I know I will have it only a few days longer. Someone from the local university will come by, puff himself up like a boy's first cigarette exhale, and tell me he is to claim the exhibited bolt for the state. He will be small and overweight and wear glasses and my wife could take him in a bar fight. The features seemingly stranded without recourse, his face will be an aquarium of disinterest, shielded from electricity, architecturally capable of being unloved. But, until then, I can let the community believe what they want to believe; I can let them climb the neighbor's rented ladder to peer over my fence at the reposing bolt, each pointing ritually back to the barely glimpsed holly and then over to the side of my house, saying, "Yes, the man lives there. He was in his underwear when he captured it!"

One day, I will write the truth about how I met the lightning bolt: the flat of the ordinary occurrence, the mere nomadic science of discovery, putting an end to my fame and the tragedy of my election and subsequent heroics. It will be a purely glass-eyed mathematical truth text, wherein I have a lightning bolt land uncocked in my yard, and I first insure there is no property damage before proceeding to what would have been a casual disposal, except for witnesses: and that is all there is to the menace, all the matter that is crammed into the myth of miracle.

But I will not write that today. Not for the electric grace of a long while.

DOMESTIC TRANQUILITY

These are things every Olomong can understand. We are not the plodding, stooped flock others take us for. We are not a laggard species. We feed the magnificent Red-Ferin, subsist on the waste they return to us, mill about in our titillating old-fashioned social groups, pride ourselves that our rookeries are superior amongst flightless species, and that our futures are ensured by the resident magic of the past. Some of us aspire.

Careworn and feather weary, we have not always had both the time and the inclination to cipher the physics of our ordinary ennobling structures, nor have we always had the intersection of idleness and ability to act on something as frivolous as thought. No one should belittle us for keeping a raptor-eyed focus on our own near-handed tasks, the nearest day's needs, and to be not looking into the next gathering month's ovulations.

But there are things we can know. Through our obsidian prism of sloganism, we can segregate entire fields of innocent knowledge and fence them into domesticity with merely a comfortable ordinary. The entire predatory muddle of cause, effect and consequence can be siphoned through the sloganeer's gizzard to come out but one tethering sentence: one mighty, balanced phrase we can sing in its ballooning brevity beside our usual mating cries and screeching, cramped declarations of territory. With this bending and construction of information, our popular entreaties roll out, though the tenets of this thought-shortening gift: as kindly as understanding, as proud as knowledge, as unstoppable as assent.

It is no longer enough to wonder: an Olomong must know. An Olomong must liltingly recite his barrel breasted affection for the lore of the flock and the flock's bountiful breakers of understanding. Now we have a common knowledge that can be passed as one set of one-sided dirt scratchings, one series of dawn summoning clicks, one burst of glorious insemination driven into the unknowingly infertile.

In the branches above, even the precious Red-Ferin, whose support gives us purpose and whose leavings give us life, cackle in imagined pride at how we have resolved our world. One line at a time, our lot is getting better. The Red-Ferin look happily down over us and despite their habitual reserve break into trumpeting song: celebration and boasting and mating cry mixed. I am sure if they could reach down to us, they would peck the back of our heads in congratulation, mock mount the most comely of us, praise the weave of our fathoming feathers.

And, profitably, there is some small element I hear anew in their joyous carnival of laughter: I think respect, perhaps, or something very near.

RED RIDING HOOD, RECLAIMED

It was a lie, but this could work if everyone sticks to the script.

So I put on my red cape and set out for grandmother's house: which is no place as idyllic as the vacation cottage referenced in all the books. No. More of a run down carriage house, spared when the ramshackle carriage barn was razed as a public hazard: a spindle of antiques cluttering the advance of the wilderness. Grandmother had set up a small living space in the back and we were always bringing her supplies, the necessaries of life. These things she could never afford herself, having raised a family and spent her youth pushing out the next shoe-struck generation; and if it weren't for our regular delivery service, the old lady long ago would have expired simply of yellow-eyed want.

So she was amenable when the wolf and I made our proposal: why wouldn't she, just two afternoons a week, take a long walk: go see the woodsman, busy herself with a little social conversation, or simply count the clouds that look like grandfather's infidelities?

Given her situation, what was she going to say?

And so the wolf and I had our two wondrous afternoons each week. His fur was the ground-water wet landscape of my emergence; I was the humbling prey that held him away from his pack. Our union was the grand gnashing of gears and pinions that only a contentious mix of species can call out of simple flesh. Grandmother's spindly bed could barely contain us. It rocked and it heaved and it prepared to give way: it stammered and stuttered and skidded on its stick legs around the room, as seemingly alive as if it had its own wants and its own surrendered barrenness. The early half of each evening after our visits, grandmother would be shoring up the bed's battered frame, sorting feather from straw, restacking her preciously gifted personal goods on the numb and rattled shelves. Fur shed in wolf-passion, in shine-tasting new woman passion, would bedevil her sheets and nothing would get the surpassingly erotic hair out.

I was drawn into the passion of fur: into the matte and bristle, the crystalline smell of its precision. The moment when compassion and cooperation turn into the single fearing purpose, the tunnel vision of personal passion: that moment I fell in love with. The blinding animal need without geometry or object. Without prelude or outcome. These for the wolf were hallowed dance steps and I was enraptured by the performance.

But there is outcome. The human half of this pair must push back the allure of the feral and look instead self-consciously into a workday future. Wolves have no future. They dance and kill and love in the present day and tomorrow is another bucket of needs and wants that hasn't yet been dreamt of.

In the practical time of women, these arrangements never last. No matter how deep in the woods, someone discovers the outlawed ecstasy; or the natural course of events conspires to break the back of a short-lived workable solution. Sometimes the unharnessed passion runs its full wicked course and the animal turbulence calms into plans for a mortgage, savings for college, the thought of a retirement to the shore. A woman begins to imagine the life she will have when the life she is having—of unmeasured actions and irregular wants and random satisfaction—loses its energy and she pristinely wonders how much love there is in sitting quietly over what is left of the morning's orange juice.

As the body cools, the omnipresence of needs becomes the tickling hint of plans. The present looks over the fence at the future.

So I am trudging suspiciously now along the path I used to fly with pleasures of rage along in days past, at the speed of bestial love and pure minded lust. Under my red cape in better times I brightly surged this way bone naked, electric at the idea of union; yet today I am dressed in deceptive layers, my thoughts as mathematical as the single purpose machine my body has become. Self-centered and demanding, my ample belly pries at the cloth and I can barely keep one foot in front of the other, my condition more comfortable with a waddle than with any other gait: one leg out to the side and the other flung inelegantly around. Gravity does not love a woman in my situation, and I feel its hands against me like a drunk fondling another drunk at the church social.

By now the wolf will have eaten the last unappetizing ribbon of my tough, leathery grandmother. I can imagine how impressed she would be that I could go back on our deal, develop all on my own a more profitable long term perspective, and scheme to use my wolf lover as my ready and unthinking tool. She would be proud at the end of her life to be worth silencing. My wolf will have dressed himself poorly enough in her nightclothes, looking nothing like a grandmother, fooling not even himself. The need for an exit of grandmother he can understand; but the nightclothes he thinks is just one more slip of a pregnant woman's roaming mind, a craving like milk thistle or dandelion root. He will pull on the thin, cheap sleeping garments as best he can and try like a man in quicksand to look the interested lover. What wolves and people do not know ensures their world stays a place of simple decisions.

The woodsman is the core to my disentanglement. His actions need to be as precise and convincing as those of a clockmaker, as true as God flinging down His alabaster retribution: His unjacketed spare lightning bolts, well timed if poorly aimed. Only in the shadow of single purpose does this woodsman know that it is his part to kill the wolf, to restore my overly complicated life to its former little girl's equation. Only he knows he is my dolorous note of revenge and salvation.

The wolf will be gone, along with his songs of completion and his eyes of a lust left lingering across species; and grandmother, with her needs thumbing the moral, will be an ironic bloat in the wolf's self-important belly. I am sick of being the expedient. I am sick of being the example that proves a tale that makes no sense.

For the woodsman's part, I have promised him his pick of my pups.

THE LOVE HOUSE

The house had always been on the hill. Dark image: brooding like a mother about to scold children caught playing with cigarettes behind the garage. It was said to have no sex, and no face anyone could remember. Its staircases were supposedly all circular.

The assumption was that gnomes and trolls, dragons and politicians lived there, eating light for breakfast and dropping dark out of their windows; that it had no bathrooms, only outhouses; and that the ghosts of dogs buried the bones of lost children in the back yard.

Interestingly enough, had it been down in the hollow, we would not have wasted a visit. Low places can be malevolent and still fit in. High places that are evil scare us with their flaunting of the universal order of events: all the more we want to climb up the porch, bang the huge gargoyle knocker, and see what misshapen errand boy of underworld disharmony answers. You expect someone like that down in the hollow. On the hill, poking its eye into the tangle of God's beard, it makes a statement.

After an afternoon of torturing insects with a magnifying glass and the great goodness of the sun, the five of us that most closely ran together as the proud neighborhood terrors decided that someone needed to see if the house were more than a painted façade placed on the hill to give our town character. No doubt, in other generations others had climbed to the shadowed porch: circus clowns had goaded brave boys into disappearing into the house's peep show dark; whimsy girls in see-through gowns had drawn thoughtless teen-aged boys onto man eating mattresses carelessly dragged into the sweetly clinging hallway.

I started up the hill, my four companions at least a dozen steps back as we leaned forward into the never-used driveway. Each switchback was an opportunity for dread, for discovery of axe wielding midgets, murderous geese or the corpse of last year's junior high prom demimondaine. The higher we climbed, the darker it got: the base of the hill full afternoon, but the top nearing midnight. The house twisted on its natural angles like the snarled shadows of competing cathedrals pushing drearily into the night.

My plan was to start at the right side of the house, hug the brick at the base of the porch, run up the eight or ten steps of the stoop, and bang on the door with the blunt end of a long stick I had picked up days before for the effort. My friends would stand still on the driveway, waiting just slightly off center, to the right and back a few paces. Their unoccupied minds would be filled with visions from late-night movies, with remembrances of family funerals, with the eyes of Laura when she fell from her uneven bicycle and one breast popped entirely from her summer top. They would be dancing on one leg no matter how still they stood.

Up the stoop and extend the stick. Poke. Poke. Poke. No one surely had been home for twenty years, no one would answer the door. I would be back down the stoop, celebrated, proud to be at an age when I could imagine using that extra inch of penis such a move would embolden. I knew the feat would fade, but it would begin a reputation.

I stood there, the pole in my hand, leaning forward just under the lip of the lurid dark deepened by the porch roof. My heart simply beat, unable to master a fitting rhythm. My eyes adjusting to the murk, I drew back the stick to make my plea incessant.

The door began to fall back, to slide ever so slightly open. From the window behind the door, across the whole thin length of the house, I could see the dark, less dark than the rest of the house, flooding in: and I was running, having missed the steps of the stoop entirely, having forgotten the driveway, grass to my knees wet and holding and expecting me to stay or fall, but I kept my verticality and bounded along, hitting soil only every third or fourth step, my troupe of four fellow cretin beggars behind me trying to keep up, each uninformed, so hitting every gravity-required contact of locomotion. And falling behind, every second farther behind.

I swear there was a face. Pushed forward, peering around the door, afraid of itself and of both the inside and the out. A face similar to mine, with the same look of bucket borne dread and purpose, but maybe three years older, maybe a few extra inches off the ground. And behind, a girl I could in tenths recognize, someone I might see in a school hallway even today, someone I think I saw all last school year, perhaps the one before; and a worn wormy mattress that looked like armies of the inept had draped themselves forever lazily across it: a mattress worn out and beaten into little more than a walkway carpet. I saw it. As if it were a still life of cattle grazing on family graves: I saw. I tasted the recognition and I could fly.

THE LIGHTNING GATHERERS

I saw the gatherers coming and I knew we were going to have a good gut grinding storm this evening: one of those storms that sends the cats under the crouching bed, and has the gutters at the edge of the roof imagining better pay and perhaps union benefits. A girlfriend slapping, fence splitting, wet-yourself-in-the-rain, bogeyman of a storm.

The lightning gatherers set up their small village unobtrusively, squatters technically, but no one complains as long as the cash crops are not trampled. Most people are standing on their sullen porches, faces forced like flat iron frying pans into the near distance, noses twitching for the scent of clouds, listening for the atmosphere's ambient water conspiring.

Lightning gatherers show up only for the most valuable of storms. They are not, in their numbers, given to collecting themselves and moving for small gain. If lightning gatherers show up on your farm, expect hail and thunder and an electrical storm that rivals getting laid in the parking lot of Dave's Strip Club and Waffle Emporium. Expect a storm like the last time your mother wore leather chaps to bed.

The rain will be as unforgiving as a gravity well, and people gather their carnival of outdoor furniture, take laundry off the line where it has been flapping unattended for three days and nights. Even the bugs go away. Pets all on their own climb onto the strength of the porch, find a reinforced space against the heartbeat of the house.

And then the first lightning strikes come distantly down, a peeling back of the far off next-of-kin dark. The lightning gatherers watch, but the atmospheric show would be too much racing up the road for harvest. They pick up their bags and stand facing the storm, the crowd of them clicking its claws and swinging its legs like a preening crustacean. They divide into cautiously pre-arranged teams.

Even as the chortling rain starts, I hang like a professional's shingle off of the porch to watch their operation come alive. It is like spying on someone else's ant colony.

A crack and finally there is lightning close enough: one of the gatherers runs over to snag it and toss it into the sack on his back. His entire hard lunged team stakes out the surrounding territory and waits, their gray pot-bellied sacks limp on their backs, a balancing head strap pulled across each pressing temple: their arms held forward like a forest of shielded wire rakes in case the strike comes down.

I admire the strength that this stance implies. I have an adolescent boy's appreciation of simple work, of effort with immediate outcome. I think: I could do this. I could wrestle wild electricity. I could clutch in my simple man's watery fist what only God can make.

The feral lightning is coming down faster now. Gatherers are running from spot to spot, grabbing the flash before it can escape, tossing it, in unpolished bursts of illumination, into their seemingly bottomless sacks. They spring about in their harvest in much the same way I would in our own harvest: we, gathering the planned product of growth robbed from dutiful soil; they, the random output of air masses in conflict. I see the kinship. I stew in the camaraderie, much like I limp around the imaginations I have of my pitching coach's sister.

The storm is over much faster than it began: there is no thistle-like preparation for industry, no arriving to work. The rain stops. The sound of thunder runs off to hide. The exhausted and smoke stained gatherers lumber back to their camp, adjusting their sacks, shifting under the weight, and having the humanity to help others whose sacks have swelled too large for one work-weary back to bear.

In the wind-gutted camps, the sorting begins. Those who did not gather wait for those who did to dump their sparking loads into the mouth of the line. These sorters are not the old women and children who could not quickly enough tussle with the lightning in the field: no, these are family members as big and bold and noble as the gatherers, merely another and terrible end of the business. These are the talon fingered specialist who refine and shape: the ones who take mere slack witted harvest and turn it into product. There is something seductive about collecting the raw material; there is something seductive about taming it.

We insignificant children, let out of our fortress houses by protective parents who are satisfied the storm has full-mouthed ended, run to the gatherers' camp to watch the lightning be sorted and the many bolts untangled. In our young lives this is the time we make choices, the time we decide who we will witlessly become. We know the horrible power of fresh lightning. We see the gatherers in their sheaths of bravery and electromagnetic quickness and their long sinews of seriousness. And we see the sorters, with their ferociously tinsel fingers and their acerbic eyes and their cruel ability to understand outputs and income and the wild shameless orgasms of judgment. We learn, and rub the flat of our thighs in longing.

Each of us keeps the secret of which type of functionary we would be, if we could be stolen by the lightning gatherers. But we will not be stolen. All we can do is carry into our coming adulthood the spinal dream beaten out of selecting which delicate part of the process we would prefer to perform, with the subtle gestures of our heroes mimicked and disavowed, with our fanciful taste of the stray energy we saw wallowing in each. All of our tinder laden lives we will be looking to apply it, to deny it, to be consumed by it, and to put it on our tables and eat it raw.

And then the gatherers go.

THE CONFUSION

These were rough, rivetless, piecework men. I stood there in my pajama pants, the night's breeze licking at the flap, shriveling my already insubstantial poke of manhood.

In the front yard the mastodon sat, looking grateful, denting the lawn. His trunk paddled the air in boredom. His tail curled up and then flattened out. His withers worked the surrounding gravity like a washerwoman at the shallows of a stream.

These men were mammoth rustlers. Big, crazy, four limbed men. The type you allow to cut in line at the supermarket. The type who insult your wife and you say: pay it no mind, it's just the way these men are. They breathe like they are angry to take in or give out air, as if any motion on their part is a concession to a world that doesn't deserve it. They hold their urine until the force of it slaps against the urinal.

I am an academic, one who looks lovingly at the world, with the world looking back and saying: I can eat you, you unnecessary product of cell division. I make no ripples. My magnetic field slips and slides about my body and has never fit right. My hands have open argument with utility. My wife has never had a climax when she was coiled with me, and hasn't thought enough of our interventions to invent the sound of one. I stumble through any ordinary social event like the space bar on a typewriter. I can better tell you what I am doing than I can do it.

But every man, even that sneeze in blue cloth, has a moment when he has to reach down to see if his jingles jangle. He has to know that, for all his intelligence and charm and grace and sophistication, he has in his cluttered cellar what he needs to become bull faced terrifying. To raise his scorching hackles and draw from the options resident within him that atavistic solution that will blow bone splitting pride through its horn like steam from a thunder well.

I said, "But that's a mastodon."

And they looked at me with that hatred I have seen in the eyes of thousands of anti-intellectuals: hotdog venders, grocery store clerks, pizza eating lawyers, recumbent girls in string bikinis, wine drinking pet groomers. But this was something more. There was just a hint of an exhale, a hint of room being left in the balloon. The shoulders of one dropped, a crispness passed over his face like an atmosphere exhausted on the moon, and the corner of his mouth started just slightly to crack out of its frame.

They both looked over at the mastodon. The mastodon, unaware of its sudden nuance, was staring at the movement of the stars, the everlasting glide that makes people believe the sky is turning, and others believe, for a second, the earth is turning. His head alone was the size of the neighbor's wheelbarrow.

They said nothing and I stood in my home's simple doorway, the light behind me, the two men in the dark, and held my ground. I could see them thinking, flash cards rising in the hardware of their brains: this is a mammoth, this is a mastodon, this is a mastodon, this is a mammoth. And they turned. They turned and started to walk slowly down my curved patio walkway, moving their feet in short frizzy glides, their hands hanging in wire ball fists, their heads bobbing like whales' heads: unsure, but moving, moving.

I watched my shadow lay comfortably behind them as they moved out of its way. The light flooded out from around me and I counted their steps as they neared the public sidewalk, turned to head back up the street, and began to move faster, their decision reached, their purpose exchanged.

I watched them go for four houses and then lost them in the yard growth. In this neighborhood, people grow things in their front yards: roses, trellises, ornamental trees, a second or third car, gnomes, mint. I had to lean forward for a last glimpse, the two of them sliding into their next task.

In the meantime, the mastodon had moved. In slow, muted steps he had crossed the recently planted six-inch hedge between my place and the pharmacist's place next door. Leaning half in my yard and half beyond it, the mastodon was nosing my neighbor's statue of a boy, almost the size of a real boy, standing in a fake clam shell, giving from his limp penis a stammering arc of processed water for any bird that happened by.

RELATIVE ECONOMICS

It is to be the execution of someone. A crew of workmen have been building the fatal platform for nearly a month. Good government work. No benefits, due to it being a temporary job—but each could apply for a full-time position, if they stand out and someone retires. We might see one of these platform builders inspecting imported fruit, or performing same-day civically approved surgeries.

It is to be the execution of someone. A small start up company has been gluing flyers to trees and telephone poles, and was putting them into mailboxes—until one of the constables told them that mailboxes were for mail and they would have to put a stamp on anything they stuffed into anyone's mailbox. So, they left the excess on car windshields, dumped a sheaf of them into the town fountain, folded them into the coin slots of parking meters.

It is to be the execution of someone. To mark the event, the hardware store is putting up a twenty percent off sale, and will give forty percent off for stock more than a year old. The grocery store next door is giving a flat five percent off if you bring in a receipt from the hardware store showing your twenty percent discount, and swear there is nothing in the transaction you might try to return. That grocery store has been a good neighbor for thirty years, and we need corporate citizens like that.

It is to be the execution of someone. I keep looking for the bars and restaurants to announce two dollar drafts, or to take up the peanuts and put out the mixed nuts: the ones you can go fishing for cashews in. A few barkeepers keep coming to their establishments' front doors and looking both ways along the street, fixing the execution structure against the time of day and the parting of the light. If enough people are out and about who will be thirsty at full price, the alcohol managers will not be inclined to give an inch. And if the crowd is too small, they won't give in either and let idlers toss back, in glasses that still have to be washed, all the profits in alcohol. No. The crowd has to be just right. They look for shadows gathering in alleys, for lone patrons where couples should be.

It is to be the execution of someone. The whole month's worth of preparations comes down to tonight. Jobs and sales will be terminated. Discounts will roll back. The talk will turn again to weather; which girls becoming women sway with a more comfortable look; speculation on when we can get up enough tax money for another execution; and what the executioner does during his long time off; and who might have seen him patronizing businesses across county lines.

It is to be the execution of someone. Enough people will gather that we will look like an audience and not just a crowd. Women will wear gloves. Children will be told not to run too far. The librarian will be out to show too much bosom, just to prove she is not a stereotype. I will be watching. I could read that book like Braille. And I will count the number of children just because I like counting and I don't like children.

It is to be the execution of someone. I am going to wait right here, on the corner left open forty-five degrees off center from the gut of the execution platform. I will wait as though I were wrestling with the librarian and fearlessly holding back—eyes bulging, pressurized forward—my already secretly sprung surging gift of children. I will be taking in the full practical view when the executioner strides square shouldered out, spins once to the applause of the perfectly tuned crowd, and then, with one hand enrolled and his business finger pointed like the bluff of a carpenter's nail, the executioner says: you!

It is to be the execution of someone. Skip, and let your heart get ahead of itself. Taste the benefits of industry, for now, on your tongue. Slap your thigh and think of giddy nights with drunken girls and the wind in your testicles and nothing, not even the disharmoniously magical, beyond your control. Think that there is nothing beyond my control. Believe that out of the remains of the execution platform tonight there will be firewood to gather, scrap that might patch a porch or lengthen a scarecrow or surprise in inexplicable ways a wife. Let everyone make the most of it.

THE CULINARY ADVANCE

All day we've been collecting the robot chickens. Just the grinning border collie and I. None of the neighbors will pitch in. They stand at their fences and smile, thinking "Serves you right," and "What did you expect?" and other clichés like those you would hear hurled from the untested mouths of boys.

Their border collies would chase my robot chickens if given the opportunity. Border collies love to work. They have thoughts the size of a human child's thoughts, without the self-interest or moral mud construction.

But we can do this alone. Already we have the flock nearing the coop, the white spit of their electricity beginning to even out, their imbedded locators starting to rile themselves into resetting transmission, into finding the mother satellite.

The sun is going applecart down and perhaps the ambient interference will loosen. Never again will I let the penning system run for days on the backup power alone, slowly bleed its strength into the atmospheric sub-spectrum. I read the manuals, but at times I am as sightless as a stone, as bull headed as melt water, and I have to fail at the technical first to succeed in the marketplace later.

The dog barks as regular as tide at one chicken frozen in place, a motor or a processor gone bad and the plump metal fowl unable to be herded, to be consummately flocked. The neighbors, still accomplishing poultry husbandry the traditional way, with flesh and feathered flocks, finds this particularly amusing: the mechanical bird stuck in space and the dog trying first the left and then the right, nose to the ground, his hindquarters hinged to anticipate a move that will not be coming.

The bird will go nowhere, but neither will any predator consume it, the weather weaken it. I can let it stay out all night, in the morning collect it and do all that needs to be done with only a screwdriver and clipboard. No loss in my asset ledgers.

The community at large does not understand progress, fights any change that does not result in lower labor costs: wedded to an economic model that paints the payments of people as the chief impediment to their own climb into sole proprietorship wealth. They hire help and watch poultry come and go, watch generations of feed get shipped in and disappear, are forever retuning the gallantry of fences. In the end, with profit margins cut in a market they cannot under-stand, they blame the hired help, cut people to cut costs, count chickens as a last resort.

Minor hiccups like mine provide entertainment but are to be expected with any innovation. See. The roosting module is coming back on line. The chickens are sparking into place, entering one at a time the coop, taking their places with searing cold happiness. The dog watches them travel like a toy train trapped, with its thousand obedient cars, on an uncaring track. He thinks he has done a good job; that he has earned his keep; that he is more than emotion and habit. I could replace him with a good electrician. But not yet.

I am willing to wait until buying season to see who is right. The executives from the big processing plants, lumbering under their consumption projections and bar chart checkbooks, will settle our dispute: the neighbors' fat, arbitrary chickens, howling and squirming, with a percentage lost both in transportation and to the diseases of cramp; or the meat of my beautifully mechanical birds, all in a row and turned with a joystick? I will tap the metal breasts of my product and regale the blubbering buyers with tails of indestructibility, Gordian shelf-life, and a freedom from serendipity. The buyers will look the spinster chances of disaster in the Medusa face, and see with me the absence of a downside.

Then, over a chilled glass of air wine, I will explain: so what if there is nothing here to eat? Cut out the butchers, the sorters, the package handlers. There is something to market, and what for all of us is any better? The matter is how you sell it: we are entering a new age of posters and advertising, virtual feast and famine. Out in my coop, the chickens will stand as a publicly known quantity: take this, and you will always have what you left with.

THE REASON

It is not just a road. It is four lanes of prime asphalt, laid down with a crown and its white lines speckled with reflective plugs that scatter the will of oncoming light. It has a slip of hard dirt between the two sets of lanes, a median where I think there was supposed to be idle shrubbery, but nothing could grow here without help. It has better gravel immediately alongside it than further out into its streaming country, but that has begun to grow away and now and again grass will poke its head up and look imperially about.

Sometimes, the cars along it are clipped so close together that you can only see through to the median in flickering instants; other times, you can peer up and down its length and there is no sound of speed, no warning shudder in the highway's shoulder, no smell of expired gasses. The peace is as awful as chicken wire left rolled. Yet, just when you think the highway is to be left alone, another car or truck or motorcycle comes hurling down its long, straight length and splits the era of the road in two: the moments before this passage, contrasted with the moments after.

I've been at the edge countless times. I've had the wind of passing cars pull at my feathers, slip under my wings as though it were to coax me to glide. I've been with seduced attention idly pecking at stones when to my backside a huge truck will approach and the passing blast of it will spin me entirely around. I remember the whine I did not recognize of the first motorcycle I encountered: the high pitch, as though it were a car caught in the equivalent of crossing not all that well a barbed wire fence, the screech of it catching its masculinity crosswise the barrier. I catalogue these things; I hold them as my bravest memories.

I have walked along the side of it both ways for as far as I could, and it is endless. No matter how far I go, the two tracks of it merge in the distance to one and then poke into a point that neither I, nor the poults of my poults, could reach in a collection of lifetimes. Walking along it is no way to understand it, unless understanding it is to be embroiled in its endlessness, in the fact that for the machines racing past on it there is some meaning, but for me none whatsoever. I do not like nor dislike it. I find beetles alongside it. I pry serviceable gizzard stones from its debris. I listen to the traffic. I rise, as though the rooster, to the rush of substance going by.

It is but the monstrosity in my back yard. I slip out through the hole in the wire, pride my way the length of three chicken coops, and I am at the road. I stop. It is a lovely road and its quality of endlessness is appealing, if acidly mysterious.

Some days I think it must be the only highway around. Other days I wonder if there are other highways, master highways that bound this one; or highways where others like myself come to the edge and look both ways to see what is traveling now, how routine the breaks in traffic might be, what fine pickings may wait in the median. Or perhaps other unknown chickenyard errants stop along other magnificent highways that are six lanes or eight, and it is only I who stops at a mere four lanes, enraptured by its sincerity.

Perhaps there are entire families of highways, entwined and dependent one upon the other, each with its own cars and trucks and motorcycles and perhaps even chickens in their comfortable wire cages busying down the road to vacations in fields of chicken feed. Roads of different feathers and fixings, which interplay and here I am at this one road, seeing only the outer edge of a larger assembly, one that makes the limitless expansion of one's pecking grounds inevitable.

Yet, this could be the lone highway of the world. There could be nothing beyond it, and the cars and motorcycles and trucks run thankfully along this edge of the world, saved by the highway from falling off into wasteland. I stand at the edge and look into the oblivion of the other side, a mirror of this side, but surely without wire and coops, without fellow biddies to share the inside out of the day with.

In most things I am satisfied. The wind of the passing cars in my giddy feathers is enough excitement for me, enough legend to drag back to the coop and pass in small, precious visions to my fellow brood. I do not think myself special: merely lucky. I draw in the experience alone; I do not let it damage my laying.

And still I have a shudder in my heart: could this sprint of macadam be simply a thing to fill my imagination to brimming? Could it be an item, like scratching in the egg stealer's yard, or roosting in the rafters, that is expected to conclude me, to make of me a finished bird? Outside of my imagination, could roads beyond this hold ever more wonder, and perhaps even bend, perhaps of me make more?

The heat of summers both empty and full rise in shimmers from the captive asphalt. If I cannot go along its side to its end, perhaps I could go across.

THE FIRST MEAL

I am shopping for the kitchen birds. They have given me a list that lingers like cold on the limits of a boiling pot. I suspect there are mosquitoes and sunflower seeds, with dandelion rough, the sustenance of birds written all over their list, and it angers me. I do not refuse their need to maintain themselves, but I know also they have an entire kitchen at their disposal. They have fire and utensils, pots and pans, and half a dozen electrical outlets. If they had the fortitude of one Burmese tiger, they could whip up a meal for all of us: a meal as broad and sanguineous as the island where the Fountain of Youth runs dry.

The list is rustling in my pocket and its very crispness infuriates me. I imagine the birds at the kitchen table, a clean place pushed into the littered flat of boxes and canisters, their beaks tap tap tapping in thought: What do we want, we, what do we want?

Never mind the other inhabitants of the house, those of us who thunder down from a night of completely round rest, believing in breakfast; or who stumble home from a ten hour day of traffic and counseling the ogres, or freezing the gold off of heresy, or combing out the long silken knots of the Prince's breath, imagining supper: a table with minerals and calories and meat arranged pleasantly. No. We count for nothing. We are residents, tenants, liabilities. The birds sit in the kitchen knowing the kitchen is the governing country, the fortified sanctuary of life, the place where is mixed the leather leash of our humbling biology.

I open the tiny list into my sweaty palm, paper by any standard miniscule and insulting and cross-dimensionally elfin. And there are the stray marks I can only assume are bird chatter, unknowable, unreadable by me, unreadable by any one: the reason I am out on this street, walking like an albatross towards the market. Step after step, driven by the necessities of the list, of the language I cannot fathom, but which is my mission's detail.

But I will be more than the man who sleeps in 4A, room and board and a shared bathroom at the end of the hall; more than the conclusion of my tidal mission. Tonight, for dinner, for all of us: four and twenty blackbirds, baked in a pie.

THE TREE SINGER

What year he entered the winding history of our gentle people is unknown. I can remember him in my earliest imaginings standing at the face of the forest—then dense and dark and damp with mystery—rounding his mouth into the force of Os and the tatters of revolutionary canticles. His words ran with barbs and hooks and unbearable line and his effort crawled like harvesting sea spiders across his forehead. Even then I could see the grasping magic in the man, and now I cannot deny the magical.

We are a fisher people. Every unaccounted-for morning we ferry ourselves out to the sea and drill it for our sustenance. We know each family of fish by name, and some seasons we bring in huge brethren by line, some seasons we bring in small takings by the bucket, some seasons we spear the fish and ride them to exhaustion. A meal of one or a meal of many is, to our way of claiming, a meal. We build with fish bone; we scour with fish scale. Our metaphors are fish; our debts are graded by gill.

The man does not fish. He is less salt and more soft than most. His fingers do not have the cuts of line, nor the puncture marks of fins. He sings down the trees. He stands in front of a selected ocean-fired, mature tree, hurling his song like a spear. He might sing half the morning, or he might sing the entire day. But always, at the end of what must be a proper time, the tree comes unbroken down. It falls with a crash of notes and a clatter of choir voices and when we hear it we turn out as one village. There is, with every fall, a canoe to be built.

The men chip into the trunk, their axes beating the unneeded wood from the ancient concept of water craft. They prepare an artisan's fire to smooth the canoe's inside. Our wives collect branches and fronds to make fish prisons: matted vessels that can be dipped in to calm water with the day's harvest still kept alive within: where it will keep until greater need churns, or until tax time, or until the insensible urge to barter.

It takes two men to work a canoe profitably through the intercourse of fishing. It must be powered past the breakers, driven around the whips and eddies of the water, stuttered past the reef. Then, to make the deftly positioned canoe of any use, the men must fish from it, entangling four hands as one: depending upon the season working the net, or the hand line, or the warbling harpoon.

Every man amongst us now owns at least three canoes. Simple math says half a canoe to each man, or perhaps three quarters so that there will be spares, is wealth enough. Yet, every time the industrious singer brings down a tree, we rush to the fall, begin the work of turning the downed tree into a workable canoe. While we labor upon liberating the canoes from the newly dropped trees, we cannot fish. In the great laughing ocean, fish pass us, unmolested. They leap from the water in mirth; they espy us with one fat eye and then spin to espy us with the other, marveling that we do not come out to catch them; to thin their numbers; to make of them better, if fewer, fish. We in our constant activity become impoverished. Want is known where there could be plenty. Only when we complete every detail of the canoe that we have been expertly making from the song-logged body of the most recent tree fall, can we then go out to fish: but to fish for subsistence and no longer for profit.

Perhaps far enough out to sea, we would not hear the man singing to the trees, nor the sympathy of the trees when they at last fall. Perhaps we could fish in peace, all sound drowned out by the bob of our small community on the great city of the sea. We would not know of the call of the trees, not cower in anticipation when we heard the singer's air rising. We would in ignorance continue simply to bedazzle ourselves with fish. But we do not go so far out. We are afraid to be beyond the catch of the sounds that circle our lives, one of which is the singing of the man who sings down trees. To hear nothing but the sea is to belong to the sea.

There are only so many trees, and so when he sings one down, we must make our canoe.

Our forest now is thin and the crash of any one tree is the death of future canoes, the harbinger of a time when we will no longer make canoes, cannot make fish prisons, and will be counting our losses of canoes and wicker against a time when none will be left, no more can be made, and we must seek the shade of a different employment.

And, when the trees are gone, what will that employment be? What will the tree singer, then nothing but a bundle of notes and unapplied magic, do? Where will he cast the shafts of his sound, and what will it transform? He will not call us to build canoes any longer. Surely he will find some other item that can be worked indelicately to prick with his ranging orison, so that we can be enslaved against it.

Until the next self-murdering task is set, we continue dutifully apprehensive in this one. And they are all such lovely canoes.

YUGOSLAVIA

There were times in the mountains I would tell the bears that years ago we were one nation with the foxes. That the eagles and hawks would share their secrets with us. Our afternoons would be spent together, all of us like prenuptial icicles hanging from some subsistence farmer's outhouse. Mornings we would bury chicken bones and our own dung in one communal hole and no one worried what species it smelled like.

Much later came the years of separation, white tablecloths versus checkered ones, the occupation of enforcedly distant lands. In the bears' dim brains the foxes' ordinary form was forgotten and became a composite of childhood closet dwellers, stray circus clowns, the man who never gave correct change at the ice cream stand. Eagles began to believe bears had sold eagles and hawks to itinerate medicine men for their inept, if magical, potions. They imagined bears on balance balls as the pinnacle in bear exclamations of superiority, the last grand bit of hubris before the bears would soon dissolve into beggar atoms.

Each then went to their separate mountains, made nests or dens or warrens, and invited me over for coffee. I was a good story teller and my protagonists would always be the politically correct animal. At the end they would share their chickens with me. My appetite was legendary, but it made me all the more a memorable guest.

The chickens remained in the valley: prey when we were one nation, prey when we were distinct nations.

Our days in the mountains passed. I had grown fat on my stories — telling the foxes how once we had been one congregation with the bears and eagles and hawks; telling the raptors how they had been the eyes for bears and foxes; telling the bears how their size and power had been augmented by flight and cunning. The chickens had been amazed

I could remember these things, and I brought them the feathers of their devoured brethren. They tried to bring thanks to their lips, but could not and simply offered me their succulent underbellies in appreciation.

But it is no more. The glory is past and these days I sleep in the farmhouse with the farmer's wife when the farmer is out hunting bears and foxes and baiting raptors. I eat the best of the chickens, but I also bring their morning grain graciously into their new pen, tell them about feather coats and the days when they were loose in the valley, with their own tablecloth, and all that it cost was a few unimportant lives, images of thanks, and a story that would end only eons away.

EVOLUTION

I have the mosquito trapped in the back bedroom. A little vitamin B laid out on the night stand as bait, and she walked right in. Simply: the bulk of her lustily swaggered after the smell of those nutrients lingering angelic in the room's quiet air. The trick is, if the door opens into the room vice swinging out, you must wait until the mosquito has turned in the room past a blocking object, until she has gotten herself out of a straight-line shot at the entry. She does not understand she is stranded in a maze of misdirection, complicated by a turn here, a twist there, with no room to fly. Some people think it is quickness that is the rock-grain in the soul; but these people quickly find out there are plenty of mosquitoes you cannot beat with speed.

Best is to have a door that shuts from outside the room; but those easy doors are usually placed at closets and pantries; and even if the mosquito can fit all the way in, you have no safety space. She can whip around on you and you might find yourself with a proboscis buried in your belly; you might find yourself being sucked hollow in seemingly industrial draws that take the mortal stuffing out of you in raging giant fist sized pieces.

No. Strategy is the key. Let the mosquito wander too far in, get wedged into the forest of furniture: let her limit her options.

Since no mosquito can turn a knob, we can relax once the door is triumphantly slammed shut: we can then listen to our own metabolisms slow towards normal as, equally, we listen to the mosquito bash her wings and her half dozen discontinuous legs against door and walls and galloping furniture. She bumps into the ceiling; over turns chairs and desks and even heavier impediments; braces her appendages against anything formidable, and tries by simple leverage and force of wing to smash through the walls. Do not worry. Their exoskeletons are not that hard.

I have sat outside a room where a mosquito was trapped, waiting there for three hours, and more. When you get one that has just fed, one that freshly exhales the fury of another species' blood inside her; one that exudes the smell of that blood being broken enzymatically down: you simply have to wait the passion out. Trap one just after she has taken down a brazenly healthy man—just shortly after she has left him nothing but odd bones and a bit of skin in his own living room— and you will find yourself waiting half a day: waiting for her predator's thrill to wear ever thinner and then eventually drift luxuriously into being as thin as a girl's Friday's night modesty at last turned off.

No mosquito is all that bright. She will tear about the room without rest, repeating, each time around, the same escape tactics that did not work on her first go-round. Slowly, her energy will fade, and the noises she makes will sidle soon duller and less enthusiastic; and eventually there will be just an occasional thump or crash or glissade of hovering. Then. Only then. Then, before she gets her second wind, you have to burst through the door and pin her with your ponderous, steel stunning pike to the floor. You have to let the blood out of her. You have to hold her to your earth and watch the breakage in biology take hold. You will feel the alien strength enraged in her fierce pushing back, the will still stranded in her to grab air with her wings and toss her contempt of gravity at you; she will make a poor man's orchestra of spirit-shaving, carbon fiber sounds: but, if you have hit her just right, she is going nowhere.

This one could turn out to be one of the long, unpredictable, sadly hardened ones. Coming uncontested down the hall she looked angular, fat, and practiced. The sight of her makes a man glad she cannot turn a knob, is not smart enough to play dead, hasn't enough free space between floor and ceiling for flight. Full on, even in the confining space of a middle-class home, I do not think I could take her all by myself: with even the champion pike I expertly use, and my accumulated years of entomological experience. Patience is my best weapon, and I will wait for her persistence at her finely glazed, poorly meted, struggling to be her worst enemy. Time gets all of them.

But, with this one, every so often I hear a rattling of the door's false brass knob. Not a turn, mind you; but it seems there is coming from inside this door a recognition that there is some complex operation embedded in the artifact: some operation that could create, for her, a way out. I have watched, and there is no turning, thankfully no turning: just a jiggle and a slap; a rocking of the mechanism; and the faintest noise of metal bearings unreservedly loving metal bearings.

No. No turning, yet. I am keeping an eye on it. If that cheap, interior door knob turns by even a little arc, my thinking on the whole of this practical hunt and kill, this pursuit and prevention, might change. My methods and bounties and public advertising might all have to be emended. And, care for it or not, with my DNA no less stubborn than any other, no less stubborn especially than hers, I might have to will myself one more step beyond: I might have to evolve. I might have to be more, too.

COSMETIC DENTISTRY

He had loved her since he first saw her sitting at the unshielded window, preparing for bed. In silhouette, the light behind her tossing the shape of all of her twilight-racer qualities out of the window, he tasted how she moved in strangely deliberate latches, night after night in the same chair, through the same ritual.

He could stand there, as open as daybreak, imagining to his long-feather drowsiness: her teeth. White, egregiously substantial: a single row top and bottom, each. What he would not give to share those spangles of mocking teeth! No hen in his yard had teeth like that. They relied on beak and gizzard stones alone. They pecked and ground the pellets, pecked and sang the praises of gravel. But not this woman. This woman was all by herself a different species: she could chew.

He would watch until the room's light was put out and the woman moved haltingly away from the public display. Presumably she slid in the dark to roost. His coxcomb alive in his sleep, all night he would dream of mastication, of overbite and underbite, and in the morning his songs to the dawn would be filled with the fine points of dentistry, the names of the teeth he would never know, never feel in his own mouth, never test with his beak in hers.

For months, his longing drove on and ever more he would see the shadow of the woman's teeth in ordinary things: in the twist of new chicken wire, in the omens of fresh stones, in the fraying of fence wood. Any flash of white was a tooth that had escaped; a crisp in the woman's voice as she tended the chickens would be a tooth growing back.

At times, he was ashamed of his fixation. He would strut about the yard, sick with himself, with his chest thrown out and his coxcomb stiff as eggshell: announcing to the brood that he had no need of teeth, no pull to enamel. He would mount the first seasoned hen he could find and shout "This I do without teeth!" and the biddy would weave and stagger under him, wishing she was not toothless.

Yet, always he would come back to the open window, the woman in profile combing her hair or clearing away the day's tick and tock from her face. Even in silhouette, in profile, her teeth aslant he could see as the most striking of her features, as the point of her beauty and the nick of her utility. Nothing else about her reeked so of value, of summation.

He resolved that he could not remain a voyeur. A consignment to the good or the bad had to be made: he had to redirect himself to the flock, or give his featheration to these, the purest of teeth. A rooster is nothing if he is not one way.

So, this night he has decided something will happen. He will turn from the window or turn to it. He will put down his love of the woman's sequestered teeth, or he will luxuriate in her pornographic smile: a smile he imagines being as wide as a hen house, as deep as the manure pit, as enticing as the chicken feed shaken with clatters of song from the bowl of an apron.

He will decide for duty or desire.

When he flies in through the open window, she has her hair brush in her hand and is beginning the thirty-seventh stroke. At first, she makes no move; but the rooster alights on the chair arm, wings folding awkwardly in, his balance like that of a man patching a hen house roof. He tilts his coxcomb back and begins to probe with his beak for the woman's gaping mouth. A quick tilt of his triangular, peerless head to the side, and he has his desire visually fixed. In her surprise, her lips clamp and she moves her head back, but the rooster is too practiced.

Off balance the woman swings with the hair brush, a round house that would send her children flying to arms length, but no further: but the rooster is too close and she muffs, accidentally brushing him upright with the side of her arm. He presses his beak into her lower lip and the blood begins to run down her chin in thin punctuation. He does not know where the teeth begin nor end, nor where they go when the woman draws the doors to their whiteness closed. He edges back to re-center himself; and she tries to grab him with her nearest arm, bringing her feet under her in a plan to abandon the chair for altitude.

The rooster thinks: I must get in. I must feel the clack clack clack of beak on teeth; I must see if they are as wondrously stone-like as I have dreamt they are: if they scratch like a foreclaw on galvanized metal, like a foreclaw on the steel of a jewel becalmed cage. I must know the casual whiteness, the length and depth of the rows. I must caress their beginning, explore their end, curve the mysteries of their length.

And, as she gets one arm about the rooster, her feet now flat on the floor, the rooster finds through the blood a gasp, a momentary parting of the lips and teeth, a warm, dark cavern: and he slips his lover's beak between the two rows of worshipped teeth, driving, driving himself forward, his claws braced on the wood of the chair arm, his body cradled against the woman: an intimacy providing a support he had not suspected, her arm paradoxically allowing him to stretch against the suddenly not unpleasant confinement.

He thinks: this is what it comes to. This is what the curious ailment of teeth leads to. Here is the power within the beauty of the carnivore, the beauty within the strength. No rooster may have the grace to be a dentist, but the formalisms of biology are not for specialists alone.

As she stands, the bird still struggling forward, she is unable to twist her head far enough back, to bring herself into consequence with gravity: her balance grows uncertain and with one step she goes down against the wooden foot of the bed, her jaw slamming wholesomely shut across the inherited mahogany. Snap go the teeth, and she rolls to her knees, choking, the lifeless bird set loose to run its last few circuits about the room. The head she spits out like a pit of the neighbor's fruit, and it goes lifelessly bounding across the wooden floor: two skips and not enough symmetry to roll to the wall, lying instead near the chair where all these long nights she has managed her hair like the prize possession that it is. The hair that her husband says is the feature that drew him to her, the element he wraps himself in to seal himself in her smell.

Deep in her jaw one top tooth un-suits itself, wobbling, uncertain of its future, keeping itself from pitching out by only the barest of intentions. On her hands and knees on the floor she can feel it become indecisive.

Tomorrow will be the search for a replacement yard master, a trip to the poultry farms that offer prideful roosters to interview along the route to and from the Dentist: the Dentist where that one uncertain tooth will be pulled and replaced with a false one that looks as hale and sturdy and as lovely in profile as the one it replaces. She will run her tongue over that new imposter of a tooth as she twists her hair in her hand, then lays it flat across her shoulder, singing to it with a new limp in one side of her mouth. And then she will brush those dark shivers of hair on the way home, using the brush she could not stomach parting with, no matter how much unpleasantness it is a plank of this night. She will give no less attention to any proud feathered strand than the strand next, counting before long out loud the strokes.

But tonight, she wretchedly coughs out pouting puddles of blood, her own mixed with the rooster's, sternly reaching down to hold back her elegant spirals of beloved hair. And after a magic moment of his wondrously frenetic, headless victory dance, the rooster simply falls.

JUSTICE

These meetings are not so secret. Just on my way here I came upon a man with a parked vendor's cart. One telescoping pole had been put up from a gadget on the cart's corner and he had a huge red bowler hat balanced atop it.

As I passed he said, "Hey, can you use a red nose?"

I looked at him without changing my direction. "Do I look like I could use a red nose?"

"You all do", he said, with a smuggler's glance to both sides. "Just some of you already have one, some don't."

"What 'you' are you speaking of?"

"You know. You. Clowns."

And I walked on. The word was out again.

It has been months since our clown meeting has been the secret it is supposed to be. So many clowns gathered in one hall can be a delicious target. There are the people who are afraid of clowns. There are the groupies, who want to sleep with as many clowns as they can. I don't mind the groupies. There are the wanna-be clowns. There are those who think that clowns have their own comedic plots, who believe our special knowledge of clownery gives us advantages we might press against a blindly serious world.

To many, my oversized shoes hide an oversized agenda. I have to be careful.

I cross the street to avoid another vendor hawking exploding cigars. He demonstrates one on the curb, with a crack and a thump that sneaks along the false brick fronts of this district's second class establishments.

Some of my ilk buy these things, and then hand them off to strangers, hoping to create a diversion, hoping that if the meeting is common knowledge, at least the exact location remains unknown. A half dozen ordinary citizens scattering in their private ways, each armed with a rubber cane or water-shooting daisy, might confuse the more casual clown hunter.

The professional, however, will still pass through.

At last I recognize the old, un-powered sign I have been told to look for, and then sight directly across the street to the selected alley. Four doors down from the right brick cornice and there, a basement entrance. Knock twice, and then sound the bicycle horn.

I cross the street and head for the door, the latches of my loosened suspenders dragging hotly behind me.

I reach under my coat and feel the calm solemnity of my air gun with its full load of deadly confetti. One of the clowns in this room I am about to enter must be the leak. We have been whittling the list of the suspicious down from the very first time our meeting went surprisingly public. I remember painfully that first unintentionally public meeting. Oh the bother! And how we had to be on our best behavior: all night riding tricycles and tripping over our shoelaces; pouring water into glasses with no bottom, and tipping glasses of imprisoned fluids that were locked on both ends; slapping ourselves with our suspenders and parading duck-waddle about in ankle length trousers. The horror of it! No true clown business could be conducted and for the unwelcome guests, it was nothing but pure matinee slapstick performance.

Even that first night, we started to look for signs of the informant. Here, a tie that matches the shirt. There, a hat that fits the head. Little things, all dubiously wrapped in professional courtesy. From the many that might be suspected, we started to whittle away the dependable. Now we all know that no matter how long the scroll, the same few names repeat.

I make sure no one from the carts has followed me, then reach into an inner coat pocket for my red rubber nose. I knock twice and grab the bicycle horn's operating bulb with the full cup of my hand, as though palming the unisex breast of an underage hooker. I point the brass at the door and slip the business end bare inches out of my sleeve.

Make ready. Each meeting is an opportunity to eliminate more of the innocent. Soon there will be only the guilty, one name on the scroll: a pretend-clown sitting in pants that curiously fit, shoes that are thinly casual and neutral in color; someone whose hair behaves.

The gun rocks slightly in its tear-away holster. Tonight, the confetti may fly.

COURTING

A person only gets to make this single broad-cloth, life-rending choice one time. Even if there is divorce, and a second or third or fourth husband, there is only one time in a life that anyone gets to have that muzzle-flash, center fire, new first husband. And, at that time, in that instant of hitch, a healthy body thinks this will be my soul mate forever. Every courting woman knows, down to the over-stretched crease of her two-sizes too small jeans, that there is no way she is going to turn out to be one of those sad shells whose first marriage attempt came down in shreds, like thin paper practice targets in a thunderstorm downpour: for years after with her limping her way half loaded into conversations and social events; looking no longer for the perfect armament, but instead pining for the acceptable, and likely to enter into the next union like a steel-stock business woman: pros and cons laid out on the nightstand, and maybe an even balance between the good side and the bad side of a union striking the flash plate as being good enough. No. At this point, it is all good. Good competes with better. Better competes with saintly. Saintly competes with downright wicked. A primed courting woman's trigger finger knows the right time all by itself. She will know her prey when he displays his full magazine, and his cold, unwavering barrel.

With this church social, the room is full of ammunition mindful of the common mating dance. With a polished stock or not, a woman set loose in the gallery has fair chance of getting a hit.

You load your hair behind an ear, set yourself into firing position, hammer back the balance of your weapon, and survey the field for targets.

With dark rim-shot hair and eyebrows a shade lighter, the fellow with the AK-47 right now seems to lead the pack. He keeps an eye on all the other cocked potential suitors, rubs a thumb along the spine of his weapon. The thumb slides deliciously where the oil is smothered into the grain. It is a bit on the unusual side, selecting a weapon made in another country, having to be wearied with keeping the seldom department-store available ammunition in stock. But it is the most popular assault weapon in the world, and the selection puts his judgment in line with some of the best train wrecks that can be seen on television news. It gives him a mysterious, international appeal. His boots look like they have seen mud in successful defense of property, and are almost certainly worn not simply for Sunday and courting. His rifle he probably chose in order to cement his anywhere/anytime image. Everyone wants to be a bad boy at this age. A slim lean and a bit of a cock to one side, he looks like he could fly into a final, no-holds-barred answer to any question at the drop of an idle invitation. Makes a woman wonder what else he has done to puff and polish his self-esteem. His elbows could hold out a while. His hips might slip right past semi-automatic and into full machine gun recklessness without even his knowing so. Dance, he eyes would say: I'm loaded.

The curved clip hangs elegantly below his signature rifle; and he has taken the shoulder strap off, preferring to hold it by the main mechanism with just one sure hand: the fingers spread like each could do unsponsored damage, alone. The wooden stock recalls antique days of natural materials, of recoil filtered through tested fibers. Bent into his own comma, he looks like he can calculate the weapon's walk when it thunders to fully automatic, and that indefatigable machine starts to concentrate on firing rather than on hitting. The barrel at times in the not too distant past has certainly left a bare trace of dirt and oil on his pants legs. He probably fires the piece mostly from the side.

Across the room, in the ghost of his own smoke, the suitor with the AR-15 is thinner, has a filet of blond hair streaming across his speckled forehead; has the straight, jagged edged news-reel style ammunition clip; and leaves the shoulder strap laid out for support. The fact of the rifle's carrying handle says he is practical, used to doing business as business. There is a creeping wiriness to him, a bubble to his shoulders that hints that his brand of thin is not a limitation. The composite stock requires him to take a bit more in the kick back, and it does not take much imagination to suspect he fires from the shoulder, letting the world know he can take it. Bet on it: he can keep the barrel nearly flat with a three-shot burst. Imagine him with the M80 grenade launcher installed underneath! Imagine him crouching, shirtless, the sweat of commitment dragging itself across his neck and onto his chest. That gun is American made, or almost so, and he wants the whole room to know it. Better or worse is not a question.

You curl your lips under, spreading thinner the ruby lipstick. You check to see that your shirt button puckers the way it did in front of the mirror an hour before. You stop yourself from smoothing your jeans at your hips. They slip a bit here and there, but endure. You have not eaten all day to fit into these jeans, and you can feel the tiniest tug on your focus, the lack of a bit of sugar smoothing out the edges of your brain. There are excuses for letting go.

The AR-15 boy pulls his angry air in through barely parted lips, regulating his soulful breathing to firing advantage: even for standing at a social. The dip of his chin shows he sees his world in terms of targets and non-targets. All business. Once again: all business. You could be that business. If he puts a hand in his pocket it is because there is something in that pocket he wants. If a woman could get him to dance, she could probably see the barest tip of a loose round left in his frayed breast pocket—maybe a hand-loaded, over stuffed cartridge: the special project he keeps with him all his waking time, and on the bed stand beside him at night.

Each boy knows the other is looking to feast on your heart. You lean in and out of the corner of their eyes: slipping into the knot and then out, a curve and a smell and a comfortable place on a game trail that could use a double-back. Each is randomly dressed in his finest camouflage; each has his weapon clean enough to eat cold beef with; each sports an extra clip in a back pocket. They have the jaunt. They have the sass. For an hour they fixed themselves to look unkempt and casual, beating out details like hammering nails into a show rifle cabinet's frame. They move their display pieces from hand to hand, lean into the weight of the weapons, trying to maximize the stature each mechanism gives them. If any man doesn't know what a particular gun brings out in him, he had best learn. No one wants to be making Smith and Wesson revolver moves when he is fondling a Bushmaster.

While the two of them compete for your attention, you have caught the eye of the stocky, street smart soda jerk with the Colt 45. He lazily casts only one eye in your direction, peering through the picket of his hair. He leans back against the bandstand for support, crosses his legs in a daring picture of ease. Sure, it's only a pistol. But that 45 caliber bullet packs a lasting punch. The wind of a near miss can almost fell a man. And he wears it jauntily in a low slung holster that falls across his hip like those Chinese-proud hip huggers you wiggle into when you decide to look openly on the prowl. He eyes you with that one ever more focused eye and lets his hand rest on the butt of his classic weapon; and your bet is that in a closed space, distances short and not a fatal issue, he could work wickedly well with that old Colt. Firing from the hip there would be that deep throated whump whump that barks louder than the grooved chamber dogs of the other boys; the other boys whose rifles have an appeal and draw, but which do whine and snap: like their testicles are not yet fully out and tend to lie a little flat, even if they will do good work in a pinch. It takes a man to pull down the kick from a Colt, and he looks like he could one-hand it, brace the brunt with the brutal muscle of his Saturday night's Sunday leather clad arm. There is something to be said for old-fashioned strength.

Yet you don't want to be seduced by the call of the past. The Colt goes back so many years it is hard to fit it into the currently proper picture of spit and swagger. These days, if you want to show you have manhood in your pants, you get an assault rifle. Small footprint, high impact. Sizzle and show to go with your ability to put out a practical stream of no nonsense. And would you want any sort of man who would be showing less? What they lack in hair on the scrotum, they can make up for with the number of rounds one lonely clip can hold.

But don't get ahead of yourself. Look around. Let your still crisp, still pretendably new blouse creak and tease and lure the hungry in. Let it get just a little darker and the beer cans a little emptier. Let the nervousness and unease work along the backs of their necks and edge into the quiver of their thighs. Wait for the night's early erections of hope to go slack. They will begin to mill about, wander in and out of each other's musk. They will watch each other with as much sex as they put into watching you. And when they run out of indoor tricks to play, they will challenge each other to something like an empty can shoot outside on the fence beside the parking lot. It will be a pop and a ping and their little brothers collecting brass; and you sitting on a car hood, your clothes as tight around you as a drunken-chance game's blue ribbon: you gloriously watching the wood splinter and a legion of blameless cans getting first one hole, then being mercilessly reused, and reused, and reused, until each ends up shredded into nothing anyone can make sense of: not quite recognizable as something forcibly enrolled as a target, or perhaps only something stray caught more than once in the field brush cutter the yardsman uses on Wednesday, rolling mindlessly in circles and squares and any geometry that pleases the way the yard is laid out.

And you will keep an eye on each of them. The stance. The steadiness. The victory dance. The apologetic adjustments after a miss. Their breath, even looking to have less oxygen on slipping in than on galloping out. How long each of them can keep his aim straight, and how quickly each tires after the can has been filled with ecstatic nothingness. And even what the game does to the can in the end: whether the beauty is gone when it is no longer a target, or whether the battering itself makes for a different, more noble beauty; how long the loveliness of the can holds out, how quickly it has to be used to be effective. At the last, rooted on the hood of the car like the knocked over signpost for Eden, you let that puckering button go bust, and hope for the best.

Better to be a spent cartridge than a misfire.

THE BEAR SEEKS A POSITION
IN ACCOUNTING

All the years I have worked as a circus bear have given me the talents I prize most. My balance from the ball is beyond the understanding of ordinary bears. My swiftness of paw is unseen in the common elements of my species. I can juggle sometimes as many as three objects as high as my forehead. I know I am only lightly batting objects in the air, my own paws unable to grasp and guide. But I do it so well that no one understands the edge of the artifice.

And yet, all these years in my former jobs, I have kept the understanding of what it is to be a real bear. I have kept always in one serrated corner of my regimented mind the memories of foraging, of establishing fatefully what of the roughage around me is edible. I have remembered always that I have no natural predators, and that I once idly terrorized the small, insignificant orders of beasts lurking around me.

I strode the line between servitude and mastery. And I realized that, in fact, the circus master with his suit and tails, his useless and simply-for-show soulless whip, was doing only the same as I. Performers. Entertainers. Even the ring master was such as I.

So why not apply? I wriggled into this suit and had my wife cinch up my drop dead conservative tie. With her sensuous electric fingers she can do things I can only watch. She patiently combed out my wire hair and filled out the initial application with the information I dictated to her from the safety of my living room chair.

I met her, if you care to know, after her fall from the high wire: a fall I broke quite happenstance, rising to the audience's feral delight on my unmatched hind legs, my front legs extended to maintain my perfect balance. My act was proceeding independently along its own, well planned course. And there she was: a blur of motion materializing into my dumbstruck arc of limbs, enough weight that holding her I could not stand as upright as my script demanded. And for no filed reason, that lovely fall was serendipitously broken in the bargain.

Since that time I have come to believe that I can do anything. And this is one of the things I can do. My strength is legendary, my luck obvious. You must understand this: when I place my arms on a ledger, magic will happen. It will be a dark, balancing wizardry that anything with a history that fits well in a department store suit cannot give you. This march of dry numbers in dry columns is what I was made for. Balance this against that, keep like objects together. I am a natural, and trained to be so. My wife says that I am quite the omnivore.

THE COOK'S ALPHABET

I am having my way with the waitress. Her dress is bunched up about her waist and her panties are dangling at one ankle, not merely twisted to the side. She is on her back and using her hands to hold herself stable on the table top, wrapping them each under opposite sides of the rectilinear surface, one foot on each of the plastic covered benches that sit bolted to the floor on either side of the counter top style dining plane.

At the moment, I have her by the hips with both hands, leaving I am sure wonderfully pouting red marks just under the crisp of her bunched uniform; and I am going at our happy collisions not quite as fast as I could, but I think with a rhythm that at this point in her shift will fit best in the long train-passing shadow of her tock filled day. In a moment, I will send one hand to clutch the fold of cloth that protects her left or right breast, and squeeze like I am trying to empty the last of the ketchup from one of those not-for-retail-sale containers sitting unused on all the other diner tables running in families of five or six both to the left and to the right.

I am as rigid as I have been in two years, maybe three, and I thank God that my shirt is short enough that it does not get in the way. My pants are lifeless just below my shins and there are absolutely no impediments to my work. My shoes, even though they have those maddening tubular ties that stubbornly defy effective knots, have yet to come undone and my toes are dug repressively into the insoles.

I have not looked closely at her face yet, and it is now tilted back and taunt at the neck, her chin presented upward as the forehead drifts back and the crown rolls under along the table: but I have the impression that she is passably pretty. Had I known I was to be so successful in my courtship dance, I would have looked more closely, reconnoitering over the lip of the menu; but I could not know. She moans and hisses and chops at the air in a way that tells me she is relatively fit, and I can feel with the flat caliper of my palms the ripples of someone perhaps 25 or 30 who has not yet begun to let gravity socialize her. I am ego driven, with just a little toxic pride in this conquest, to stretch my demanding pauper imaginatively deeper, to be the grand buffoon whoremaster this achievement would have me be.

I wanted poached eggs and a side of cheap steak. The almost null diner at two thirty-seven on a Wednesday morning seemed alive with its prowling emptiness, and I was sure the grill would be cold enough to cook the steak all the way through as it warmed and stuttered of dusty butter being used as the only non-stick agent this splatter of an American icon would need. That enabling butter would sit a while unyielding and intact, until the heat would hesitantly gain ground and the ladled butter would then begin to dance and hiss and burn tomorrow's stains into the service metal.

But there was no cook and the waitress with coffee in hand asked what I would have and what could I be doing out this time of morning and when I told her what I really wanted—a reason to be in a diner at two thirty-eight and maybe even two thirty-nine—I found that is what she wanted as well and I have always had a talent at tying unsequenced needs together into a small sterling nothingness; and so here we are, together. I am trying to breathe as though it were directly connected to what I am doing. I am trying to keep her from sliding too far along the well-used table top.

Imagine Mom and Dad and little Billie at Sunday brunch, a Rueben sandwich for Dad, a salad for Mom, and Billie triumphant with burger, fries and a shake. Chocolate, probably. All in this booth. The waitress, perhaps this waitress, bending over them: asking if there are enough napkins; if the mother, consumed with her excited black-hole of a child, would like a fork the dishwasher had done a better job with. Their pernicious bottoms pressed into the seats where the waitress now presses her shoes for leverage; their meal arranged on the table top in the precise logical order necessary to minimize wasted effort as the food was consumed: the table top that now the back of the waitress's unimpressive uniform unknowingly wipes clean. The salt, the pepper, the sugar, the ketchup: all for the moment gone, replaced with other equally random needs.

Had the Formica counter been covered with a tablecloth, it would be now like a bed with a sheet — and the backs of the plastic covered benches would be like pillows, and this could be a cheap two hour hotel room, and our efforts a different sort of performance art. In this experience art, when another customer unexpectedly steps in he stops at the door, looks down the row of empty booths to see us at our worst and at our best, the two of us one animal measuring how far it can run in its pen; and as the waitress, who I will call Rosie for the rest of my life for no particular reason, arches her back and lets out a straggling, yellow-dog-in-the-trash moan, he looks back at the door which has closed behind him, hesitates a respectful moment, and then steps back out, walking slowly to his waiting car, the steadfast engine still warm from his arrival.

With the barest of acknowledgement, the cook peers around from the detached storage locker's thinly cracked door and sees that the exiting man is wearing leather shoes and what appear to be woolen pants; but the cook can see no more as the man leaves, and so settles back against the flesh colored wall, returning to his comic book. Tomorrow, Rosie will note how this happy hollow of a cook will sometimes recite the alphabet as he silently reads his comic book, and that it keeps his breathing as smooth as the fur of the thunderous alley cats who flourish in the scraps. He handles his breathing just as delicately as I am controlling my schooled workman's breath now. She will, tomorrow's afternoon, remember singing the silly alphabet song as a child and will hum it silently, reflexively, wondering if the cook ever sings it as well while he is cooking.

I am no short ender, no slack-jawed benefactor of the simply convenient. I hold up my end of any bargain. Breathe in; hold it until all the oxygen is sucked from even the underside of the air; breathe out. I am mumbling the name of a girl I tried to date in high school, maybe even a cheerleader, maybe a spiral notebook poet, or some other rarefied, tranchet, unattainable collection of womanly parts. Raven hair and a bust too good for me. R is for raven, R is for Rosie. R is for

Rosie, R is for raven. No part out of control. I breathe in and think I can hold the air on its edge forever, but there it goes: a stream, no matter how hotly fired, that barely dents the volume of the room; and I know that A is for appetite and A is for apple-wood bacon and A is for after and the coffee has gone cold, but it is now two fifty one and the cook unbundles himself from the storage shed, folds his comic book into the broad pocket of his apron, and prepares to check in at three.

THE DAUGHTER
COMES OF AGE

The wife does not respect my traditions. To her almost any tradition, no matter how honored, is nothing but a habit, to be thrown out when a less bothersome habit can replace it. With her, any process is about the plodding march towards utility, a cheap maximizing of outcome, a means to a dishwater end, nothing more.

I see tradition as a source of pride, and a comfort in itself. No matter how much work completing your task in the traditional way might be, there is a truth about an achievement achieved in the same back breaking fashion as would have been relied upon by one's father, one's grandfather, one's great-grandfather. My wife prefers shortcuts, a prepackaged life. I see what we are, and how we strive, to be in an ever deepening debt to the species.

Not that I mind improvement in the drudgery of our daily lives. But roots matter; and so, too, the solid sounds of familiarity.

I look forward to rising each morning and walking, while breakfast is just a plan in my wife's slowly clearing head, the near-genetically known steps behind the house to saddle Tessa, to walk her slowly to her own edge of wakefulness, spinning in well worn ruts around the open floor of the spider shed. I do not resent the time spent brushing each of her legs. I cherish the routine of settling her riding blanket across her back and then sliding on the saddle and buckling it securely beneath her abdomen. I end up knowing, from the simple utility of my acts, more succinctly just who I am.

The wife is always on about motorcycles, about free range two wheelers that can run whorls around a spider-mounted man. Noise and smoke and dirt. Repairs and gasoline and city licenses. Sure, cycles can range farther, sit idle longer—but they cannot handle the rocks; climb a near vertical grade; or stare down, with a predator's warning eyes, an anxious and tippling herd.

Motorcycles.

There is no feeling like patrolling the edge of a herd of market spiders towering idol-like on your own mount. Motorized, you flash past: something going by in a blur, and the herd to you becoming nothing but a collective with no specific point of reference. Spiderback, you can stare into the undecided eyes of each member of that herd, watch for the quiver of a spooked spider and turn him back into the social group with subtle, simple moves that require balance and opposition and the counterweight of a plurality of legs. You can sit quietly and listen as the clicking of his mandibles slows from self-rescue agitation to a mindlessly-apt belonging. With undulating patience, you convince the spider herd it is an exorbitant spider pack, and so it stays together and travels the roads you subtly drive it to want and understand.

Motorcycles?

My wife packs my lunch as though it were merely a job; some days, after she has been proselytizing for change, she assembles my mid-day meal with an anger that still shocks me, a focus that cuts a line in the patriarchal passages of my cherished profession. She knew what I did for a living when we married, and in our courting we fiercely coupled more than once balanced on spiderback, a threesome as diaphanous as silk webbing in a draft of dark evening mist.

Motorcycles!

We move the herd from hunting ground to hunting ground, letting them take all the crickets and beetles and flies they can harvest. We transfer them around paddock to paddock, each fallow field filling again almost overnight with insects and larvae and the small mammals that a herd can return to. The wife should appreciate that in this phase of the spiderherd's life, all hands are home every night, our mounts sleep in our spider sheds, our appetites spin at our own tables.

Our market spiders grow fat and careful and we begin to think of the drive to the rail head, those two weeks away from home, my sleeping nights wrapped against the belly of Tessa, my black and yellow mount, her legs folded in about me and her collected silk emboldening my nighttime warmth. Each day is a diorama of spiders on the move, a herd pausing only to feast: a ribbon of scurrying, seeking the loading platform where each arachnid will be marked and added to the great caravan of spider filled rail cars heading for the packing plants of the heartland.

I make a good living, paid in base wage and commission. A month after the ride back home, I am parceled my bonus from the home office, based on seniority and the total pounds of spider meat the packing plant reports for our brand. Salary alone pays the rent, and with my bonus I am a generous man.

Yet, my wife, in defiance of my heart held traditions, supports my reed of a daughter in her relationship with the thin, reedy cricket from two streets over.

The girl is barely old enough to know the hammer and nail relationship of the long, ritual scurry towards coupling. She has learned the woman way of drawing her prey in, but not the essence of capture. This age in her will pass, and her skills sharpen to properly pursue this all-consuming use. But for now, she is entranced when the boy stands on the sidewalk outside, rubbing his spindly legs together, creating that godawful racket that keeps me awake, and has Tessa scraping the sides of her stall in the spider barn, leaving the cautious marks of her memorized longings against the reinforced brackets.

I try to be the reasonable father, to understand the girl's independent testing of the velvety edges of rebellion; but I cringe when the boy refuses the indulgent side of spider we offer him on those evenings the girl insists we have him over for dinner. Leg joints and spider-eye salad are not to his liking, and I have to settle into the Internet to see what a cricket eats.

Aware of my predicament, I try not to watch too perilously when he lazily runs an antenna through the web of slack golden hair free at my daughter's shoulders, then glances stunning bare inches down to imagine what small joyous things lie just underneath the press of her shirt. All of her querulous body quivers, untested, as he attempts to appear full grown in front of the father of the girl he has yet to learn how to master: as he tries to run the edge of my opinions, with all six of his misjointed legs firmly planted between suggestion and innocence. Winter is a world of disasters away.

And then the wife starts talking again about motorcycles. Types of engines; and how small a down payment is needed; and how the insurance is actually less; and how the machines wake each morning instantly with the turn of a key. She twists her wrists like a rider asking the engine to announce its mechanical masteries, tilts her eyes as though laying out to take a curve, and putters with her quick lips the sound she thinks the mother of all motorcycles would make.

They are in this together, and it would serve them right if, after an early evening constitutional visit, I left the door to the spider shed cracked open just narrowly enough for one business-sure mandible to eerily poke out; for the breath of the spider within to flick in and out of the door crack, so close it hardens the dark. For that one night, at least, it might scare the dreary, world-thickened leg scrapping right out of the boy.

But the girl must come to her own conclusions. With four limbs or eight there is a symmetry that a daughter might build a future on. Six is a suspicion, but it is she that must become suspicious; and I must wield my patience as though I had placed around its ventricular complexity a legion of my own trembling, disappointed, and yet darkly hungry, spiderkind.

CONNECTION

We pull another one out to take to the infirmary. It is the usual ritual: unplug his device from the wall, make sure the battery takes charge, place him in the wheelbarrow, whisk him to the holding area, then plug his device back in. No one wants to trust the battery any longer than is necessary.

I tried to carry extra batteries at first, but then realized there are so many brands, so many makes, and all are not compatible. It usually is not an issue. Long ago these patients went to keeping their devices constantly plugged in, and the batteries are always fully charged. But, every so often, a battery is bad, or went so dead long ago that it could never recover, and when you pull the plug from the wall, the device dramatically goes dark.

Then the otherwise somnambulant patient suddenly bursts into emotion; howling; looking, for the first time, at the assembled recovery staff; pointing in terror at the cold and stunningly quiet device. I have had to transport one of these patients. It is no fun. They can go from agitated to violent with a shimmer in the transport, a bump in the road, with a cough from an attendant. The trip is one of racing behind the wheelbarrow as you aim it with the squirming occupant about to come out from both sides at once. I have heard of patients dumped into the road, grabbing at the hint of a device in a team member's pocket, imagining devices in the street, concocting devices in the shrubbery, in alleyways nearby, in the reflections smiting homes along our weathered path.

Team members are warned to leave their devices at home when an intervention is necessary.

Even these suddenly disconnected sufferers, when finally in the long house we call our infirmary and connected again to village power, calm immediately down, flex their thumbs and forefingers, peer into their devices and begin to click and whir: their bony digits going like the claws of crabs picking over the best of the carrion that has sunk into their depths.

No, for this patient, the battery kicks in, there is not even a momentary flash of recognition, and he is boring through his caverns of e-mail, twisting in and out of his closest thousand friends' delectably shared pictures, reading and forgetting his news feed, sending and consuming vacuous brief thoughts, joining: all while we are rolling him at the best speed achievable through public streets, citizens and visitors alike stepping aside, the wheelbarrow leaping and loving the ruts and bumps and potholes, his body quivering with each ripple in gravity. He will do alright. He will be delivered.

A stray dog barks at us with no conviction at all. The dog has seen this before. The dog knows he does not matter at this moment; he will pick a better moment to matter tomorrow.

When the devices first appeared in the village, we knew this could happen. Enticing were the brilliant covers; the felicitous ring tones; the finely frail finger driven screens; the warmth of a secure and calming connectivity. Why, the false sense of importance these devices provides can be intoxicating. It can make a man or woman seem, in the context of the electronics, much more than he or she might be able to muster at a neighbor's fence, with laundry behind on the line, or the thatch for roof repair balanced under an arm. And we could imagine—some of us could, even at the beginning—that, fueled by insipient narcissism, these devices could lead to unbridled social paralysis.

It is all this data that fails to rise to information; this wealth of exposed circumstances that fails to drive the warmth of understanding.

It is no matter to me. I wait for the call: another victim, thin, seated in the last of his or her provisions, fouled with his or her own waste, found in a home or office or shy corner of a public spot, calciferous thumbs clattering away: eyes unblinking, the tiny screen reflected in the stricken subject's eroding and nearly spent pupils. I am a volunteer. I check to see whether it is my night to drive the wheelbarrow, to put on my protective jacket and heavy shoes, to make sure my device is connected to its charger in the bedroom: and I race puffed and proud into the street.

It is a small town. My mates pull up alongside me. We run to the coordinates we have been given.

I do not know what they do with them in the infirmary. Every time we drop someone off, we see the many we have dropped off before, clicking away, drumming with forefinger page to page, eyes locked into short scanning movements. They are cleaner; they are seated for easier observation. They no longer soil themselves, or the attendants clean them more often. I have faith something will be done for them.

But I also worry that there are fewer of us. At one time there were a half dozen teams; now, there are but four. And some of those four teams are missing members; some have been called out to carry one of their own to the long house that we have imagined an infirmary. There is no sadder moment than to be one member short, and that member to be the patient in the wheelbarrow.

There will be a cure. I can feel it in the weariness of my wrist, the arthritis at the joint where my thumb becomes pleasant with my hand. But many of us have made a pact. If there is no cure, if we lose more team members, combine teams, become one team; if that team then grows too few to haul the diseased to the house of isolation and hope— then the one that remains will cover himself or herself in mourning clothes, and will skulk to the edge of the village where the power company generators squat, pushing modernity down to us through heavy black lines.

Those lines can be cut, or the fuel pipe exposed and bored, or a rod passed through the generator blades. A brief shudder or a clang or the spitting of metal and the deed would be final. The village would go dark and brooding, waiting: save for the screens fed by the devices' fully charged batteries. But those would go too, in a while. And that one team member left—himself the entire team, the last villager with his feet on the ground and the winking of air consciously lurking about his lungs—would wait with both of his or her marvelously guilty hands desperately covering wounded ears as the wailing rises and the deconstruction begins. Perhaps that one faithful team member might remain long enough to see his once fellow villagers lose their electronic sense of invincibility; to see them look down at their own withered arms and legs, and parenthetically stand, and besotted with misdirection attempt to walk; or perhaps even notice. Or maybe this savior will run, run—fear, bold text, flowing through him — thinking now that they are alone, what will my bereft compatriots do?

THE VALUE OF SCHEDULE

This morning is a breakfast of delicate, missed timings and unscheduled outcomes: an effort of animal need, and an unwelcome act of the ordinary. Breakfast is an event I have no plan for.

Last night I left a woman tied to the train tracks one county up, and a single dark forest over. I was going to give her a good scare, frighten the quaintly moral resistance right out of her. My intention was to come back in time to untangle the Gordian knot holding her to the humming rails; to draw her up in my farm-country sturdy and seemingly repentant arms; and march her straight back to the ramshackle cabin I had arranged and decorated just so as to make her ever so easy at ladling out a serendipitous dose of unknowingly unwarranted and undue gratitude sex.

That mixture of evil, threat, repentance, submission, innocence, salvation: we could have been the feral force that causes streams to run backwards, that propels predators to kill for the practice alone, that seeds the undeserved plenty of some half human species, and draws changelings into indentured labor. I would have feverishly sucked the light right out of her.

Then the train came five outrageously flat and unremarkable minutes early—so there I sadly was: left with only unworkable pieces, even the knot mowed into frayed threads, no salvageable part of the sensual corporality remaining: already the carrion picking at the wonderfully vermillion shreds left by the intersection of cartoon evil and the dull and irrepressible physical ignorance of modern locomotion.

I am not naïve. There was always the possibility of a watch being fast, a schedule unexpectedly changing: in the end, the needs of the collective workflow outweigh my private plans for personally pleasing propositions. I accept that. I know that the true evil of the world resides in the fact that there is no evil: only physics and chemistry and no guarantee of coordination, no promise that the gears of one or the other will intermesh with the gears of absolutely anything else. I have to take my failures along with my successes. But no failure is to be welcomed; no failure should pass unlamented. A sour mood this morning is the least I can summon.

I think of the girl, screaming her ice crystals of disbelief and, at the last, kicking like an unthinking bull in the competitive ring, certain that I was still coming back: in fact, looking for me to appear on the ridge, my plans reconsidered, my heart changed, my character enflamed by her helpless matinee-worthy condition. She would have, with an open mouth and predatory eyes and sliver of cold on the inside of her thigh, believed anything at the end. Without that stabilizing belief there would have been only the stock locomotive; the rails heating up as their rewarding friction approached; then the ferocious finality of her charitable bonds. And then smack: no believing at all.

And the very next unrewarding day: my breakfast. Three eggs poached. A half loaf of artisan bread. Some congealing morsel that might be the red left eye of a gorgon, or the hump of one of the neighbors pigs who pays for my services in trade. The chamber cook, that slander of indefatigable motion, brings in the dishes as though she has been bringing in the dishes for fifteen thousand years. She has been employed to do it but five thousand querulous days: a woman of strange gravities and mercurial moods: cheap labor, but expensive in the excesses of dry, sexless air around her. She simmers of methods and manners no one knows, an enigma of practical procurement and preparation: the source of what I do not care to understand or acknowledge. I know of her as much as I need to know. I am left paying wages to a woman I would never tie to any tracks, never bargain with for any delectable cross purposes. I am left on slanting mornings like these with simply a woman who sustains me, one I would not corrupt even if I knew the key to her corruption.

I missed my good opportunity. Once you get a victim kindly twisted about her metaphysics, consumed in crystal values and sodden outcomes, she is primed for your meticulous base adjustments; she—or he—presents herself—or himself—as raw material, mined from the common ground by a rough process involving many incorrigible hands, and ready to be refined by yours. There are no alternatives.

First order when I have my soul readjusted is to check my chronometer against the town clock, check the town clock against the stationmaster's watch, and ensure the deadening line of civic engineers have all the same calendar readings. Neither good nor evil can occur without a measured playing field. Nothing happens outside of our dimensions: nothing happens entirely on its own, beyond the ever clarion cleaving of time into seconds and minutes and hours and days. Until we agree on the sequential substrata of all of our trials and irrelevancies, opposites cannot contend, and no particular moral crime can return us to our stingy origins or shove into the unshaven face of our futures. We are adrift.

I will stop by the watchmaker's before lunch. If I remember well, he has a daughter: a daughter rumored to be a dangerously forbidding sprite: diaphanous, as light and simple as the edge of idle thought, as the plug of action into consequence, as the uselessly sculpted lingerie of logic. Perhaps she can learn, too.

SUSPICION

I have had that pen since I was a child. It is my favorite pen. I've filled it with new cartridges more times than I can remember: and who does that these days? Pens now are as disposable as the words written with them. Out of ink? Chuck it, take one from work. Take one from the courtesy counter. Take one from a trade show booth and advertise while you scribble.

My thoughts are not simply of finding the pen, of seeing it returned to both its place and endeavors: no; I want to punish the thief. The idea of the pen's comfort and utility has gotten wound up in the sense that only retribution restores balance. Not only must the pen be reclaimed, but the act of its taking expunged. I do not think I can write again without order being re-established.

And so I set off down the street with a description of the thief: a huge, bulbous head ending in a beak; eight arms or legs, half left, half right; each limb covered in suction cups. You do not see that every day on a city street. Rubbery to the touch, if you venture close enough.

The housekeeper should never have let him into my study. I understand her appetites, her need for those eight arms to wrap seductively, seditiously about her; to feel the scrawl of his ink on the paper edge of her neck; to listen to his erotic clicks and fathoms; to feel the bare mercury of his suction cups on her periwinkle skin. I begrudge her nothing. But he should have stayed always downstairs, come in and out by the service entrance, and kept out of my study.

But, as I think of it, I notice the loss now only because it is my favorite pen. It is the one pen of the hundreds that contain me, and the one that immediately I would see as missing: the clarion. I can imagine, now, how many ordinary pens he may have, during his courtship of the housekeeper, taken wistfully into one of his arms: then palmed that coveted pen completely, and made out before the housekeeper suspected.

Perhaps all along the affair with the weary housekeeper was just a ruse—a way into the house, an excuse for lingering. How many spent cartridges can he have left tossed in the street around this house, how much ink could he have spirited?

By now he will be half way to the aquarium. I must hurry if I am to catch him while he is still possessed of the beloved instrument: the ink still running in his chowdery veins, the empty body of my pen yet in a tentacle, ready to be abandoned in the roadway like the cheap girlfriend you have enjoyed and merely pushed out of the hotel's fourth story window. No such fate for my pen. No. I will catch up.

THE SCARECROW

I drive the back roads. No one places a scarecrow on a major highway. It is the small, backyard gardens that have all the scarecrows. Of course, small is relative. Most of these gardens lie in the nature of one hundred yards by fifty, and in some manual labor is supplanted regularly by machinery, even if it is only hand driven machinery rented for only the first week of the season. More than a stray meal is expected out of such land. These family gardens are warranted to make a few meals all by themselves, and supplement nearly every meal with something fresh, canned or pickled.

Too many people tie pie tins to lines in the yard, expecting the wind to kick up enough clatter to keep the birds at bay. Some add spangles and whirligigs and strips of crosscut cloth. I guess it fools some birds. But it leaves only more for the dining birds that see through this ruse.

And I've seen some remarkable scarecrows. Sure, some people put no effort into it. They put a bag on a stick, cross tie a twig that will not last beyond a couple of dedicated rains, run one of the children's old school shirts through and through, and let the confabulation twist lonely in the wind. Some try to get away without the shirt, or the crossing stick, or paint a face on a board.

I've seen others, though, that you can almost strike up a conversation with. With painted round faces, and straw hats, and a polished pair of shoes. A shirt that looks like it came out of the wash just hours earlier, with the starch still stiff and singing in clothing folds. At times, scarecrows like these will be bent forward, man height, leaning as though a proper farmer to hoe out the vixen weed threatening his summer corn. At times, they will seem to be leering, daring the fowl.

I came across one dressed out as a woman in shorts. The bosom high and erect, the legs stolen from a manikin, I began a manly reaction before I got close enough to notice the stuffing at the edges, her mouth forever resigned to its unchanging expression.

No matter. I shoot them all. I'll park at the side of the road just ahead of where I want to be, slip down along the high grass by the fence or along the drainage ditch, edge up to where I can slink through the length of the garden. I'll poke my shotgun through the hanging produce, take center aim, and quietly squeeze off an explosion that tears the monster into a hundred air burdening pieces. How I love that ball of ballistic ejecta, almost like a mushroom cloud, with bits and pieces of straw or padding or shreds of flannel shirt pelting down in the ordered growth, settling into the rows; and the lighter stuff drifting, drifting out over the rest of the now empty garden, across the border with the back yard proper, perhaps into the netting of the screened porch.

I don't stay long. The family is usually out onto that porch or out of the backdoor within minutes. Places with gardens large enough to support a scarecrow spread their noises thinly, and peppering anything with a shotgun at close range will draw a small crowd of the nearby located. Not a few farmer's wives, and farmers themselves, have found themselves hollering at my backside as I leap over rows and hightail it straight for the woods or the road, making an indirect route to first, get away, but then get back to the car unnoticed.

The first ten scarecrows were the worst. I had to learn how to find them, what areas most likely would have a good crop of seasoned scarecrows: the kind worth shooting. Then, I had to experiment with distance and gauge and choke and get the right stance for an effective shotgun blast. I learned to adjust for the apparent construction material of the scarecrow, the interference of growth nearby: what to do with wooden supports, what to do with scrap metal tubing; what to do when the garden was planted right up to the scarecrow's arm pits, or instead grew around him with a respectable buffer of wickedly wild weed.

More than once at the beginning did I linger long enough to stare a garden owner flat in the face, to be seen fully before I turned to run. A couple gave chase, and I learned that they know the bends and twists of their land far better than I, so I had better for the future get a good head start on my exit. You can only learn these things in the field, and then you figure out how to keep yourself in a straight line between hitting the mark and successfully getting away.

It is more than seventy-five now. Different types, different races, different sexes. One was about eight foot tall when I nailed him. Another was just a midget, a scarecrow I nearly missed and would have missed maybe another two weeks into the season. I don't play favorites. There was one dressed in a business suit; most are covered in last year's jeans and a shirt that came as an unfortunate holiday gift to someone in the garden's tending family. Many look like they just finished chatting up bored wives at the trailer park, a cocky lean against easy pickings. Some seem happy where they are, and others look like a change of venue would do them unceasing good. One looked perpetually surprised, like my coming had been foretold to him, and his face had long ago frozen in the act of astonishment. The weary looking ones bedazzle me.

Sometimes the birds lead me in. They will circle a good scarecrow. If something scares them off, they will linger at the edge of that fear, looking into the eye of what keeps them hungry. I look for the black congress just ten or twelve feet into sky, or gathered on an open bit of grassland beside the mathematically enciphered cultivation. There is a good scarecrow about when I see those gatherings. He may be buried deep in the undergrowth of the garden, or pushed up against one end, but he or she or they are there.

One day, I know the time I can finally be satisfied with all I have accomplished will come. One day, probably a dreary one with the hind teeth of the cold trying to hook about my underwear and the sky sucking in its face to pout of ready rain, I'll be sneaking through a row of squash, using perhaps two stands of corn as cover, my prey scarecrow spotted, fixed just a few yards off, almost within range. I will crouch down and slowly edge the business end of my shotgun through the corn, ever so slowly beginning to shoulder the brash gun's butt. There will be just a crackle, and the last of the day's listing light will hit the barrel from just the right angle and, whump, that scarecrow will come off his stand and hit the ground running. Boy, he will show he has heard of me! He will be off like the sound of murdering crows, feet barely touching the ground and stray pieces of him not properly stuffed into him leaking out between the buttons of his shirt. There will be little more than elbows and a shuddering rear-end, the trademark of escape.

I know I will simply stand there in awe, thinking finally this is the one that got away. Finally, one got away. He, she got away.

I live for that day. I can taste it like straw lovingly drawn across my predator's tongue; smell it like the sexual smoke of gunfire mixing with the atomized remains of lesser scarecrows. That wonderful day I can feel even now, working its will in my testicles, waiting to leave its singing wet spot on my tense trousers. I am letting sacred air out through the holly wreath round of my ripped-bark lips even now: O how lovely in freedom are the birds!

JOY IN THE SENSE OF PLACE

I can't remember when they first became separated. My earliest remembrances are of selecting cases, different characters of cases, each for a specific purpose. One case would be fur lined for winter; one would have just a thin mesh so it could be waved in the wind, not too violently, to allow the air to flow through on thoughtless summers and whisk away sweat. I had to have the hard case, protection against workday hazards; and the soft case for lounging, elementally relaxed, yet certain of protection.

Of course, when I am home and unlikely to be disturbed, I set them loose on the table. I have a slightly curved decorative dish that lets them roll to the center, uses gravity to ensure that they are not by a careless bump or tilt accidentally set free on the floor, to roll under the furniture, or unseen into the walkway. If you have ever had to move a dresser just to find one that has rolled under its edge, you will then soon master some method like that helpful dish to keep track of them.

I've not really missed the attachment. At times, not having them in their usual spot is a comfort. I don't get anything caught on the cutting ridge of my pants legs' divide. I don't sit awkwardly and then find myself squirming for a better geometry. Loose shorts are not an issue.

But then again, you have the problem of how to carry them with you. You certainly do not want to put them in a back pocket. I tend to put them in a good, firm case in my shirt top pocket. Briefly, I used to carry them in a sack tied around my neck; but all the jostling, the banging about my torso, the sudden shifts side to side, made them some days sore in that dull, distant sort of way, as though they were sleeping and drearily unable consciously to wake.

The main problem with this detached circumstance is sex. Not the accomplishment of it. No, my main engine still works. I can point direction without hands, make a place to hang my underwear, do all the things any fully developed man can do. I am willing to say I am even more gifted than the average male who is surely out there looking to drive his species imperative into some crisp and lovely female garage. But women react to the absence. They look right past my steel straight primary motor, and see the neat V where my legs unencumbered join—and their mouths drop open, and they let out a whoosh of air, and their eyes look to lean out of their lids, and the whole focus of my intended evening changes.

Even before they drop into wonder at my omission, I will already have the case on the night stand, ready. Closed of course, warmer than usual, but still secret, buzzing with thoughts of what hopefully is to come. They each shudder when the night's partner starts to point at the place the happy two were expected to wait, fully loaded and counting on release. And if I take them out of the case, thinking to try to hand them to a woman: half the time she will shriek one of those cartoon mouse shrieks, both hands drawn up and back as if in surrender during a robbery, as though she has never before seen a pair liberated. The other half of these attempted affairs she will barely poke them with the flat of a finger, mumble something about communication. Too often, far too often, it all ends with the prospective mate becoming dressed too soon, entirely pre-coitus, apologizing, backing towards the door while I stand there offering the two of them, the rest of me already beginning to go limp with rejection.

The key, I found, was to pay for sex. Most of the working women I encountered had seen a great variety of need, and were practiced and willing at an hourly rate to adapt to the situation at hand. I would contract someone through a mutual acquaintance, or an Internet add, using round-about language to say in five hundred words precisely what we needed to say directly in perhaps a hundred. Cash in hand, I would meet my business partner at a mid-range motel, then just inside the door settle all the particulars, and, as casually as the gravity might allow, explain my circumstance.

In such a setting, given the pure mechanics of the transaction, there would naturally be more curiosity than concern, more method than misapprehension, more reason than rejection. Cutting out the emotional—and, on the hired woman's side, the passion—I found made for a pleasing difference, and that sensation in itself became a bit of a sexual edge: sort of the sharpness of an axe considered before the cleaving. More than one paid companion asked me to see them before they thought to undress, and it heartened me a little to find my situation something of interest to someone whose interests should have been purely cash and carry.

I would sit on the edge of the rented bed, my still connected instrument of wonder rising just above the skin of my leg; and the rented woman would sit in whatever chair the room provided, with the case I had just handed her still closed. Slowly, I would tell each woman, open it slowly. And they would move in tiny gestures, unclasping the catch, and slowly opening the ornate case. Both of the severed wonders would be inside, aquiver, filled with lightning and ready to strike. Cautiously, one woman might blow lightly across them, what little hair that might be left on the scrotum standing eagerly up. Or another might draw small circles across them with the flat of her pinky, or let them roll gracefully into the warmed palm of her hand where they would swing about until settling in the gravity sink just behind the commencement of her fingers.

I would sit there, stiff as a rock jutting into the ocean of the room, contemplating not so much this naked woman that I had contracted to meet my most elemental of needs, but imagining what next she might do with what she regarded in the case, or already had slipped yearning to burst into her palm. To press a bit of lipstick to the pair, or drag the tip of a tongue slowly across, would have me writhing on the bed, purely without thought or being, without plan or soul, my wonderful devices in her control wonderful yet again, no longer so distant, no longer separated.

And one night, not so long ago, there was a new woman, one who had perhaps seen this before, who seemed to know the currency and calamity of my condition. The case emptied into her hand and the contents regarded, straight away she squeezed. Fingers curling around and the bottom of her palm acting as the backboard, she squeezed and she held while increasing the pressure. Her smile laid out into a straight line and she watched as I slid back in the bed. I grasped the vacant lot where the two of them once had lived and I rocked, the purity of fire licking me loveless; I rocked as I felt myself go full throttle and the little flecks of gray pain I had long known must exist began to gather at the well of my eyes.

My back then bent in terror and my skin sung and my skull grew porous with a multitude of different little winking horrors. Her hand, with my omissions within, was becoming a fist. Her forearm was twisting with the effort and her teeth contested one another as ever more of her flowered into the one closing hand: that hand, that fist by the penultimate moment held out at arm's length in the direction of my semicolon body senseless in its blue writhing.

Harder, I was thinking, harder.

Harder.

MANUFACTURE

I found a jacket. I did not intend to.

Yes, I could have walked away. It was an unremarkable jacket. Brown. Medium, most likely. In wear seeming mid-life; not the best the jacket's owner owns, nor the gullible jacket he wears only to rush out for the paper on mornings too cold for t-shirt heroics. Comfortable. Creased with the details of living. The newness beaten out of it, but its utility still intact. A favored stain only the owner notices. The smell of a wife and two—no, three—children. The wife faithful, if a little under used; and the children all good students, college in the blood—and one day a companion jacket like this one.

I could have left it there. It had gone well limp against the geometry where a building escapes from the sidewalk. It was not yet soiled or abused—it had not been there long. Surely, a man was simply careless. His arms full and the jacket momentarily loose over his forearm, he had been distracted: he had been in a hurry. The jacket, unmindful of its prized position, saw an opportunity for imagined adventure. Yes, I could have walked past. The next person along, or the one after, or the one after that, might have harvested the jacket. Or it would have gathered itself ever more into an indecipherable tatter, weathering wherever the wind husbanded it, an anonymity along this street: becoming first old, then old and unrecognizable, and then some gray morning at last annihilated.

I rescued it. I scooped it from its unwise brush with oblivion. I felt the weight of it, the substantiality. I could feel its mission. I could feel its regret. I could feel its unexpected need.

Cautiously, I looked at the inside. The size tag proclaimed 'large', and I was immediately elated. No medium, this jacket. The liner was common cloth, but it was still a liner. And that liner was a shade darker than the exterior. I patted and looked, but there was nothing in the one pocket. I felt around in that pocket for some time: if there were no wallet, perhaps there was a strip of paper, or a discarded receipt, or a business address. But no. Nothing.

I boldly held the jacket at my arm's length. By then, I was committed, and I did not care what those walking unnoticing around me might think. I held it to my eye level by its curious shoulders. As it hung so, only the lower part of the back toyed with the breeze. Its arms stared unimpeded down. The collar spread out stiff, and proudly elevated. I had the jacket's attention.

What could I do? I was now a part of the jacket's life story.

So, with a bit of a flourish, in proof of my unwavering reason, I slipped the jacket on. Yes, over the one I had on; over the bunching sleeves and the pleating of the back and the chilling pull of the finicky and flashy buttons. And it came on with nothing more than this momentary displeasure of my existing jacket—which was but a dress jacket, frail in its intentions, and not at all one of my favorites. But, for all its flaws, it did fit strangely well within this newfound one.

You see, my size was but medium.

Then off I went, the jacket a bit long, but my walk left undivided. Maybe the owner, distracted in the afternoon crowd, would see me in his jacket. After I acknowledged his perplexity, we would stop and talk about how I saved the jacket. He would help me out of it with exaggerated gestures, arms held before him, his smile clean but with a limp. Over his forearm again the jacket would comfortably go. He would mention where he procured the jacket, and I would be surprised that I shop at the same establishment at times of excess. He would stand there praiseworthy, not putting the jacket on—out of respect— tilting into our conversation, relieved, and along all of his edges appreciating. I would protest the depth of my part.

Maybe.

Or perhaps he will see me tomorrow, as I come out of his favorite subway tunnel, or spin brazenly through the corner where he lounges in his favorite coffee shop. Or he might see me as he drives his stellar children to a private school where I know the head nurse, or where I have seen and been frightened by the janitor, or where I am sure I have imagined silly satanic rites are held regularly in the basement.

But, for now, I play the jacket out across my bed, thinking: what a fine jacket! Not too fine. Well worn, worn well. A jacket with life left in it, and with life woven behind it. I will give it a brief brushing. I might press out a memory of its cowering against the transition of sidewalk to building, soothing each unnecessary wrinkle. I might at the last spread it agonizingly open over the back of the chair predatory in its pouting at the border of my bedroom. Or I might leave it commanding the spread atop my narrow, clamoring bed: clamped casually to the crisp covering, ready for me to crawl in through a bare crack in the sheets, a jacket ready to have its way atop me all night long. Chances are that tomorrow, I will wear the jacket. I am almost certain of it, and the air between us hums like the promise of dry cleaning, the power of haberdashery, or the princely sex that only serviceable clothing can give to princely ghosts.

COMMERCE

When I sold my dragons one at a time, it was easy to bring them into market one at a time. I would throw a blanket over the wicker cage, each wallowing dragon calm and unsuspected by potential customers. I would walk through the crowd, swinging my ware beside me in time with my gait, as happy as a young woman walking the muddy streets barefoot with magnificent shoes held in her hand.

Most people knew what I carried. Those who had not purchased from me knew someone who had purchased from me. Dragons for soup. Dragons for pets. Dragons for security. Dragons for show. Dragons for ornamentation. Dragons for revenge. Those who have suffered dragons knew me best. Though I claim no responsibility for what my customers do, I am nonetheless known by the tragedies they visit upon their neighbors with my wares.

Business was good, and I carried dragons as though each were to the core unique, transporting each in its wicker cage that I made myself—and still do—from my warehouse to market. I waited for a sale, each customer peering into the cage—not too closely in case this dragon spits—imagining what can be done if he, the shallow pocketed customer, might have his own dragon. I am still asked about upkeep, feeding, the proper disposal of scales.

On all these matters I am an expert. I am no huckster. I try to match an eagerly nervous customer's expectations with his or her ability to manage a dragon, to fit a dragon comfortably, to establish a dragon in the family or in the arsenal. I walk my customers through the rituals of ownership, the certain shadowed signs of regret, the shoveling of fertilizer. I hide nothing.

When a sale was made, I let the customer take the new purchase, cage and all; and I, back when my tasks were committed one at a time, would begin the long return track to my warehouse. Sometimes, when there was another customer already electrically waiting—perhaps the one who lost in the bidding for the last dragon sold—I would run: headlong towards my dragon stash until I would go out of breath and then double over in rack of oxygenation; I would stumble the rest of the way, not myself again until I had reached my warehouse. I then, relying upon my assessment of the crowd and its frenzy at the moment, would select another dragon for sale, cover his cage with any available blanket or tarp, and start back to market as strongly as I could.

Most trips, a constant feature of commercialization, with his broad, overfed body leering with providence, the wheel and cart maker would greet me both in and out of the market. He might lean his wickedly corporeal presence against a substantial beam or table and roll in his tattered fat fingers the commission for a cart, palming in the other hand the frolics for war-greasing wheels. Sometimes, he would have a small demonstration cart with him, holding as cargo perhaps his lunch, or someone's daughter exchanged so the rest of her family might arrive on wheels.

He has been famous for carts as long as I can remember. Carts a man can pull, carts a dog might pull, carts for oxen and donkeys and wives. Carts that can hold enough wares to fill all of a market day in one trip. No one complains of his workmanship. No one faults his designs. No one disparages the lick of the roll in his wheels. He smiles with the curl of a mouth that could eat entire forests.

It is rumored that the road maker is his half brother, and that he shares a wife with the harness man. All of it is his business.

I expected to hold out longer than most. Every dragon folds its wings alone in anticipation of its trip to market, settles as quietly as a puppy played out. They are no bother to carry. Moving them one at a time had been my way since incorporation. But I knew I could learn to stack them. I knew my wares would adapt to being one of many in the back of a cart, rather than a lone precious delivery. I knew I could handle the dangers of mercantile progress: the schemes my dragons might come up with when cluttered together so brotherly in a common conveyance. I made preparations for the worst of it, considered security, safety, the dynamics of dragons en masse. To be in the society of dragons might be more of a dangerous thing than to be in the company of any one dragon. This, and all my other misgivings, I elected to forego. I thought I could turn precaution into a fair line of cost, toss it in with all the other particulars involved in a dragon's sale. And I could do it to great success and profit, gathering enough wealth to go about town in bells.

Forgive me, but I came around. With grander sales, more dragons can be supplied to those who can afford them. The dragon's sense of dragons grows sharper against their more economical numbers. Dragons will populate more villages; leave their scat in more vegetable gardens; consume an incautious cat or playful dog, or perhaps a fashionably stupid child or two. From a nuisance, the community's dragons will soon be a plague.

But I know it will not go on forever. What was sustainable one dragon at a time will soon be unbearable by the cart full. Here I am, with stacks of dragons each in their still hand made wicker cages, encouraging a customer to choose one over another, encouraging a customer to consider the quality of dragon, now they can be compared side to side, and not the effect. Stacks of dragons, families of dragons, dragons in every backyard, as soup for every table, as ostentation on a peasant's thatch roof, or loose in the sky and preying on common sense and reasonable expectations. I see the omens for both rapid gain and eventual glut. Too many dragons, and commerce will turn away from me and my utilitarian wares. It is how business works. I will have to sell the cart.

What galls me is that my profit in dragons will sustain the wheel and cart man. He provides a serviceable product, one that rolls almost at command, and which can hold a stunning number of dragons. I have no complaint of his workmanship. But such modernization will allow the community to ruin me. I accept that fact as a given market rule. Yet, surely there will be a short, thin edged window of time when the land will be sick with dragons, and I will be rich enough that what is bled from me for the wheel and cart man is a sum I can for those moments abide. Both of us in commerce will for that brief interlude between the gnashing cycles of business be happy. At least until someone's fresh dragon, to my delight, finds in the drearily otiose wheel and cart man an unpardonably easy source of calories.

DIMINISHING RETURNS

When we learned that the local cartel was buying heads, at first everyone thought: how silly—where would we find heads? But the mortician quickly came to market with a cart load of relatively fresh heads, and then everyone thought: why, someone would have idly buried that wealth!

The work then began of unearthing recent burials, removing the heads. Elderly to child, natural cause to mayhem, plutocrat or the working dead. We had not been given limitations on what heads would meet market designs, so we sought them all. At the start, we worked in groups, forming corporations of head collectors, setting rules for work hours and lunch breaks and a common quitting time. We carefully dug into graves; gently removed the lids of coffins—preserving the nails and tearing as little of the lining as imaginable—and labeled each head; then made sure the body went rightly back into its box, the lid was meticulously put back and faithfully secured with its original nails. Some corporations had specialist crews just for re-internment. Gatherers that were good with a shovel were as respected as the harvesters that held talent with the scythe. Pride, accomplishment and respect emanated from all aspects of the work.

But then came the lone wolves. They stealthily swarmed in, combing the cemeteries after good people were abed, breaking the lids inelegantly from coffins, removing the victim's heads with a sputter of axe; and then they would be skulking off: the body left exposed to the rain and dew and neighbors' dogs, with no thought of public decency. They came wild with the thought of profit, operating in groups of three or four, or sometimes of one. We would arrive the next morning, thinking to farm a length of cemetery row in our civil, regulated way, only to find it pock marked and holed and any degree of commerce already without the least of manners drawn out of it and gone.

Who could compete? Artistry and kindness and respect sometimes simply cannot compete with a narcissistic will. So, we streamlined our processes, cutting corners, hacking the heads from corpses as fast as we could and moving on: the headless resident of the grave tossed about in his or her box as though hit with a summer's hurricane; with the lid split to shreds in whatever manner would best sunder the building material, our heavy equipment making quick work of even the most precious of everlasting departure comforts.

Public and private cemeteries were farmed, and parties drifted out to the outlying estates, peeling back the land around family plots, overturning the earth where unmarked graves were rumored to wait. Many of us began to worry what the cartel might consider a head. With fresh burials exhausted early, some people were coming up with nothing but skulls. After a while even the skulls began to seem ragged: hunters bringing in little more than jawless rounds of bone and passing it off as a head to anyone who would not know better.

More than one enterprising charlatan tried to pass off one busted skull as two separately discovered gatherings of remains, and pretend with all appearances of honesty that the find should be considered two heads. These opportunists would take the complete object before reaching market and pop off the jaw, laying it out separately from the pate, assuring everyone that this was the best pickings to come out of two distinctly different, stingy graves. The hopeful huckster would persist in the deception even when anyone could pick up the jaw, pairing it with the skull fragment it had been broken from, and show how it fit like man and wife.

There are only so many dead people. Graves disappear with time and the housing of better industry. We are not skilled archeologists, but working class folk: those who know what they know because it is told to them by people who make profit on the ignorance they sow within us. We had only so many blue prints on how to locate unobvious dead. Yet our town is like any other: it has its criminals, its lie-abouts, its drunkards, its reprobates, its non-believers: all of those that no clean citizen would miss, and the town would be better off without. We are as forgiving as any close-knit group of common laboring people might be, but here was the chance to kill two ideas with one edict. Soon we had fresh heads for market.

No one knew why the cartel wanted them. For years they bought our produce, sold us our land and implements, took away our wives when we were tired of them, accepted our house animals and sometimes our children as tribute, explained the limits that affixed to town sovereignty, and assured us no harm would come to us if we met our end of their contract.

No harm came to us, which might be why there were so few criminals and reprobates and drunkards and lie-abouts and non-believes to harvest marketable heads from. It was like trying to bring feed corn out of a dry, sandy soil. Even with widening the definition of the undesirable, that broader definition for unexempt citizenry can only hold so many. A few of the industrious quickly made off with the available heads and we were back to the business of exploring unprofitable shadows for more.

The money had been good, and a man's take would beat most day's ways of laboring. Shortcuts can become contagious, comfortable. With everyone happy and the dead not caring, this industry was sure to go on.

And we thought: go on how? Everyone has his or her opportunities. A lover is most vulnerable at the end of a love affair. The neighbors' children are least prepared when they think they are safe. When the worker beside you is fixed on the ground that he thinks might hold an unmarked grave, he is then the easiest to prune. A husband or wife curiously entangled with ecstasy can muster no defense. The possibilities are as endless as the imagination of anyone who has painted himself in self-justified chicanery to engage in the brutal contest of daily commerce with his or her fellow citizens.

Add in a town's rivalries or feuds, envy and injury, and the circle of available heads grows ever wider. No one can forgive every trespasser: injustice can lead to profit. Just to be ready for all the ugly, brief opportunities you have, a man or woman needs to carry a sickle strapped to his or her back, the handle propped up like a comma thinking semicolon above the shoulder for quick access.

I have been won over to the new line of thinking, and can do my fellow head-seeking competition one better. I come to market with my light basket held close, looking up at myself as I make my way to the exchange station. My head rolls about against the wicker and I have to balance, just so, to keep the eyes first on me, and then on the road ahead: making of walking and coordination a surly mathematics consumed with projecting direction against the tether of my own shadow. I smile at the man from the cartel when I reach his collection station and I tilt up the basket to see that he has a full cash box. This head should bring more than any other that I have delivered before, more than any of the many heads that I have dropped in the bottomless barrel just at the edge of the barter table. More than any two heads combined. It needs to. I will have to live headless off of the proceeds for a long, long time.

OUR MONKEYS

We have been told we cannot eat the monkeys. They roam through the village, climb into people's houses, carry off our food even as we sit before it. They take our clothes from the rocks where they dry, scattering them throughout the gardens and porches and rubbish heaps. I am no fan of the monkeys, but I am told we cannot kill them, we cannot fool our hunger any more with our brethren monkeys. It is not allowed.

For generations, we hunted the monkeys. Not in great numbers: they are too small and agile, they feed too few and are too much work to bring down. No one would form a party to go hunting for monkeys alone. Always the monkeys were an afterthought, a serendipity. One would be spotted near camp, or thieving at the edge of the village, and a man with his near relatives would go get his advantage—the bow— and only one time out of five bring back the monkey. The meat was soft, the brains a delicacy, the testicles a miracle of preparation with the right cook cooking rightly.

More importantly, the monkeys feared us. We were a monkey predator, a rival who left holes in their families. They might on occasion steal from the margins, but they avoided the main. The chatter of monkeys was always far off, unnoticeable almost until the land ceased to be the village and became again the other.

The man from the district governor, however, says we may no longer kill the monkeys. The tourists do not like it. And we need the tourists to provide the capital to turn our village into something that is not our village and which the tourist will not pay to see. But the plan is given: they will stop paying only after they have paid enough that the government can make the village something not worth paying to see, free and clear. It is not our plan to understand.

But the monkeys respect us no longer. Only this morning, I awoke to find a monkey asleep between my wife and I. I started and the monkey screamed and the wife leapt from sleep like a fish out of a bath tub. She and I stood in our night clothes, agape as the monkey howled like the broken bride of a murderer. And then the wife began to chase it with a broom. The monkey would scoot ahead of the broom, but would not leave, and it took my tossing the once perfectly stacked kindling at it before the monkey would leap soullessly to the window sill and out to harass some other villager who carried in his thinking the former taste of monkey at breakfast: a taste that can no longer be played.

At times, monkeys will gather in the round of the village common and begin their monkey dances, declaring for all, in this way, that the village is theirs, that the trinkets they steal are theirs, that our houses and sleeping mats are theirs, that the fires we make in our dung stoves we make for them. At these times, I charge anew the animal wick on my bow, or rebind where the bow notch is fortified so as not to split, or hunt in the hinterlands for better, more arrogant arrows. In their hearts, our brethren monkeys know that in my heart I know I will never taste monkey meat again.

Then one day there is a newborn missing from a house well into the warm of the village: a boy barely old enough to be named, a boy who would be the third son to the son of a man who is legendary for his family's marriages, the alliances he can make through his own spawn. When the blood is found and the trail turns to monkeys, we pull our bows from their secret hooks under our roofs' eaves. We gather our arrows from dark corners of round houses and hum praise of stiffness low to the wood. We count our children and sing sorrow with the family that has lost this barren opportunity to further its name.

But before we can strike back, there is the district governor's man, ferrying a crackling greed of monkeys in his truck, saying to us: tell the story. String your grief like monkey innards about your words. Rend publicly the sinew of your language and the history of your brotherhood with monkey. Make of everyone a listener. It will excite the tourists even more, and ever more of their uselessly rich brethren will come. You and your monkeys will need each other only a few miserable seasons more.

ESTABLISHMENT

At eleven hundred, local, there is a bit of jolt and my bootstrap program begins loading me from on-board storage. The battery disconnects, fully charged, and my systems start to go through their calm self-diagnostic. I take some interest in it: I was a store clerk before I was repurposed into a barkeep. Some unpurged part of the old me takes notice of which subsystem is being scanned now, which set of bits is shouting in return to a call to alarm. I pull up the list of chores I stuffed yesterday into protected storage, and calculate that I have enough time for all of it before opening.

I carry in from storage an extra case of the better lubricant, scan the bar code to update inventory, and check to see if we have more. The automated storage bin tabs back that we have three cases left, enough for the week.

I make sure all the electricity leads are plugged in and glowing in each of our three cabinets. One is city electric; one is non-nuclear city electric; and the last is renewable resource. Each is a step up in price. Above the floor, each is fed by its own shielded incoming line; but, if you trace through the floor and into the back wall, all three plug into the same draw: city electric. Customers pay for an idea, and it is an idea they get. I'm not going to contract to have separate runs put in here for those squeamish about nuclear energy, or morally tied to renewable. But I set the prices as though I had.

I dust down each table, looking for films of lost lubricant, then scrape off the absorbent dust. If the dust does not fatten on stray oil some cranky customer absently left on the table, then I can put that dust back in the can and use it tomorrow. It is the little savings that keep a place solvent. I need to be creative. I can use dust until it actually makes itself wet with something. I once had a can last me four weeks. It will eventually clump just out of residual humidity, but it is easy to know when it has lost its utility; I know when I have to woefully crack the seal on a new jar of it.

I am a machine marked by thrifty subroutines.

I check the leads at each table, making sure no pins have been bent, and that the gold has not worn through. I look along every inch of the USB cables, making sure nothing has gotten kinked, or by some patron has been rolled over and the sheathing left wearing through. I try to make the tables wobble. I look for metal shavings that have gotten wedged in the floor.

It is a long list of preparations. I bet my original operations load was shorter. The simple act of learning fills a lot of otherwise happily idle bits.

Last I look in on the air baths. Overnight, their automatic cleaning routine should have pushed them to run empty, cleaning themselves out. But you never know when some farm worker with two days of manure head to foot will gum up the works, and even an overnight cleaning cycle might leave a fine mist of animal goo on the back wall.

I do what I have to do. Before I open, I make sure the place looks like an establishment you would want to spend money in. Good lubricant, good electricity, air baths that will squeeze every bit of the day's drudgery out of even the most asymmetric machine. The place screams a cut above; it pulses luxury; it texts unchallenged that it is the place where the most expensive models hang out.

And that's what draws in the working types, stumbling off the factory line, taking this opportunity to play at being a few editions ahead of themselves. Their money is good, and the tricks to getting it all the easier.

I signal the lights to come on. The sign outside says "Open", and I wait behind the bar, watching the front door.

First in, always, are the drainers: squat little machines that have been scavenging all day and are just about out of battery power. They come up to the table they always claim over in the far corner, and without asking I pop them each a lead of city electric. The balances on their pay cards vary, but they always seem to have enough to get a few jolts of the cheap stuff. For the safety of my other customers, I check them out for hot spots. If they have been down in the radiological waste bins again, harvesting re-useables, they could be putting out a few stray particles that might make a customer's execution register skip an instruction, or randomly flip a memory slot 1 to 0 or 0 to 1, and all sorts of confusion get set loose. I don't need those complaints.

Some owners don't like them in their bars, but their money is good.

Tonight there are four of them. I will not let in a group much larger than that. From all the stray light and power and rusted radioactivity they scavenge through, they can get completely out of alignment and then start arguing amongst themselves. The more in the group, the more likely one is to go half a clock tick off. It is almost fun to see them fight over the contents of a memory location, knowing all sides to be wrong. But there are breakable things in here.

Next, the night's first couple walks in: a man of about 35, with a domestic administrative model. A rare mixed couple. Not that mixed couples are rare—it is rare that they are out in public. The administrative machine is a newer model, one with the fresh antigravity stabilizers and an independent cortex that hovers just an inch above the rocker that the man would call a neck. The machine is configured as though it just came from work: hull coverings and exterior make-up to make the device fit into an office environment that is pretty heavily seeded with biologic types. For me, I wish they would dress a little more sassily to come in, as it might perk up the business a bit, but I really fail to care.

The man leads the machine to a table near the back and, impatient, walks over to the bar. I can see this is his first time out with one of the top-of-the-line models. A smart man would have arranged himself around the table, taken advantage of the few moments I was giving him before I would have walked over to take his order. He could have settled himself, gotten his heart rate back to barely noticeable, and unhurriedly considered what pride of mannerisms would seem most comfortably familiar in his planned engagement with this device, in this place, with soon surely other devices around and all plugged happily in.

Some biological units just don't seem to have quite the understanding we have of what it means to be data based. I've still got 'man to man, machine to machine' somewhere in my off-line storage, but such slogans are not considered proper any longer.

"Evening", he says too loudly, his nerves apparently about to crack. "We should start by topping off the battery. I'll take one electric lead, please."

I bend slightly down, causing him to do so as well, in reaction. Keep them focused on anything but sense, I've learned. "What type?" I ask, seeming to be talking directly to him, though I know the machine he came in with can hear everything we say.

I have one eye on the drainers as they settle back and hum. There is a drop of something, water or oil, or worse, just underneath one of them.

"Type?" he asks as flat as tin. He seems to fish the simple word from the underside of his tongue. He may be older than I thought, but no smarter. Thirty-seven, maybe; and perhaps a salesman by trade. A haberdasher. Or, from his dress, a bulk produce purveyor. Second generation, at that. A man whose hands are always looking to hide in his pockets.

There is still only one drop by the drainer. No worry yet.

I bend even lower and he folds at the waist to follow me down, bending almost into a formal bow; until he slips one elbow onto the bar and breaks the symmetry of the moment. I can work with this geometry. I shift into the most conspiratorial voice my speech processor can create, dropping my volume and letting my sound chips grow cold. "Listen. Go for the renewable. It is a little pricey, but it seems to knock the delay out of the power transfer, gives just that half nth of barely perceptible pure performance. With a battery full of that, the machinery unplugged will still hum full bore all night long."

So he orders the renewable, swipes his blue-vital credit chip across the reader set in the center of my forehead, and takes the wrapped lead back to the table.

That makes for a good sale, and the night is off as smoothly as an exercised differential equation. I adjust myself to the other end of the bar, keep one set of eyes discretely on the drainers, one on my first night's couple, one set on the front door, and in background I tell the air bath master control processor: be ready.

And, just like every night about this time, in roll the three organic-leftover processing machines from the plant on the corner: none of them bright or pretty or ready for detail work. They can trace their line directly back to the first programmable trash compactor. Their collection spoons are still rattling at the ready, and their main memory is still filled with tasks of just a few recognizable steps; yet, deep within their dented shielding, they know they came in to upgrade, to be for the night less of a drone and more of a bon vivant. I wave them over, cooing "okay, okay" and line them up at the runner along the base of the bar, pull out a data access cable for each, plug them securely in and begin the slow download of the personalities they will rent for the evening. When their memories are full with tonight's novelty identity, I will get them ready for a go in the air baths. Time enough in the morning to be dullards with a job and no concern for fine maintenance cleaning.

Sometimes I think I am a nanny and not a barkeeper.

The drainers take an interest. Sometimes the upgraded machines can put on quite a show. The drainers are too short registered to be able to calculate accurately all the twist and turns of the simulated personalities the new customers will get, so often they watch the customers interplay and bet on the outcome. To them, it is almost pure chance. They could be no happier with anything else that might sizzle their sensors.

I catch the man watching me as I coil around a cabinet and check on the download speed of one of the leftover processing machines. If he has been to a recharge-and-lube bar at all, it has to have been one of the uptown joints: a place little more than a roof and a row of sockets, a common spray of graphite, and one left-leaning air bath barely in the back. A sign over the door with one letter out. By the end of the night, that administrative model will have him wrapped around its overflow buffer and he will be singing a wireless ditty into what he thinks is the device's auditory input station.

I wink at him, just so he will know he hasn't gotten all there is to know about the affairs of machines figured out yet.

Yes, I am hospitable with biological units, but I always remember what my first owner would advise: always best to turn off the higher functions when dealing with humans. You are not they, they are not you. Let them deal with the mechanism, not the code behind it. Wise man. I think he had a few cortical implants.

The door flies open and in steps one of the huge salvage drones, followed by one of our local biologic bit-rats. The drone's collection tentacles drag behind him and will be sucked back into place only when one of his periodic self-diagnostics reveals that they have been left out again. The three machines at the bar, not filled yet with their night's prickly personalities, lean away from him and try to go into shutdown mode, but the load program prevents it, and I have no worries. I point to a table across the room from the first couple, giving the machine purpose, otherwise the salvage drone would stand there all night. With direction, it moves solidly over and I bring the brooding behemoth a fisker of industrial grade graphite and two cheap electricity feeds. This sort of machine is not all that bad when you get used to its constitutional abruptness. They have a personality for cannibalization, and once you take that into account, they are not that disturbing a lot. I don't mind having one in, keeping the other patrons focused.

I'm hoping for a better crowd, but it looks like I'm filling up with scavengers. I'd like to see a network cabinet assembler come in with its production line mates. Or a solid, multi-tasking dog groomer. Something I do not have to keep an eye on.

The bit-rat walks right over to the man and says, "I have an over-ride routine for this model", and I can never tell how a happily engaged flesh and bone customer is going to react to a bit-rat. These are the low end of human-machine interaction spectrum. Bit-rats always have an angle, something harvested, something salvaged, something that elevates privileges or runs in an unsuspected buffer. They hang about the salvage and the maintenance drones, looking for patterns, recording the squeal of memory chips. Being so unabashedly biological themselves, they seek out the biological units that wander in, and the interaction is more parabolic than geometric. But I bet this customer buys. I bet he pays too much, and I bet the override works. You hate to see them waste their money on access when they could be wasting their money on maintenance, but I can't control the bone and protein crowd. I've yet to figure out their programming, and I stay out of the mathematics of it when two of them are dealing.

But I've already plugged into the memory space of the man's companion, and I don't know what he thinks he might be getting. A surprise, most likely. His high end model companion is computing pi, to hundreds of thousands of places, in the background, just to keep its circuitry warm.

The bit-rat shifts one leg to another and gets as close to the man as it takes to make sure the unsure man comes straight to the conduct of business, if it is conducting business he will do. The two of them look like bookends on a shelf with no books.

And then the man looks directly into the bit-rat's curling and gloriously greedy eyes and, pointing with a slightly arched finger to his finely tooled and processor stacked companion—companion, yes, but still skin to core machine, top of the line, sealed-factory produced—he starts by saying, "She ….."

And the whole place goes as silent as core crash, as still as a busted bus: with the air as empty of vibration as the first nanosecond of a shameless reboot. Not a blip on the wireless, not even a synchronization pattern. She. The whole place takes in the excess of it. She.

But only for a moment. And then the inexcusable is over.

I keep the flash pattern that runs through my cache down in cache and not into execution: Look buddy, it's a machine. We all know it's a machine. Why don't you look at it and see what it is?

The man looks around a brittle half second; but the room starts again its small cartography of whips and clicks and grinds and untraceable sounds, and each machine turns back to its next instruction. The man's faux-pas unrecoverable, the bit-rat backs slowly towards the door, his hands inside his coat and his eyes barely focused on anything or any place: the hoped-for transaction now only an imagination that will probably wait warm in his skull at the end of the street until the man and his companion slither out and try to make it unseen to public transport.

The man eyes each machine, but none looks back. Their programming has moved on, and his thoughts just turn round and round like a drone's wrist unscrewing a hinge with a hammer. I almost feel for him, him and his awkwardness. Almost.

And that processor studded administrative model simply unfolds one delicate arm, lays out the finely tooled omnigrasp, and teasingly taps the table top to get the man's attention, beginning in its harmless depths at the start of pi all over again.

SNAKE OIL RIGHTS

1.

I love driving this type of country. The rolling hills. The houses set way off, with porches pushed protectively out in front and continued welcomingly along the side. Grassland mostly, wheat and corn and hay, spotted now and again with a favored tree. Little road signs that point down two lane intersections saying that whatever-name bluff is two miles that way, and implying that, if you go there, you will know it from the fact that the three houses there are closer to the road than the houses you now pass here, one or two stranded in every half mile.

The grade is not so steep that I really hear the rig labor as we go up, and on the way down I can coast without needing to hear the break kick in. The rise and drop is never long enough for there to be a complete loss of momentum going up, or a surly exchange with gravity going down. You know you have been up, and you know you have been down, and that is about it. The autopilot doesn't even think of warning you.

My companion in the side seat crosses her omnivorously smooth legs, slyly. The thunder of her spiked heel nearly touches the floorboard as one blue sensuous snake of a thigh slithers carefully over the other, the lip of her mini-dress folding just a little back. I turn to look over the whole of her and it takes commitment to this trip's firm schedule not to stop the truck and move into the back for just a bit of rumpus. But I need to make the next little hamlet within an hour, and I know what this woman can do. I designed her. I even designed the clothes. She was one of my early models and, even though I have moved on at times, I come back to this set of attributes, this collection of abilities. I am particularly proud of the swept back ears. I get a lot of comments from people about that. Sure, everyone remembers to make the eyes more of a slit, and angle them slightly up. But to continue that angle with the ears and slip them back behind the plane of the neck: now that was pure genius on my part. Too many have tinkered with the basic human form and come up with a freak no one wants about the house; but I know just where to stop, and those ears are a thing of beauty.

I need to get to wherever this place is that has been for too long expecting me. I am the new novelty, straight from the complicated cities and now out in the hinterlands. Even in small little farming communities, where people have to come in from thirty miles out just to do a day's shopping, they are seeing progress these days. No matter how badly they want to do it, yokels cannot stay yokels. If they try, their own children abandon them. I am bringing progress, modernity, the life they see on their quaint hand held view screens: so, like or not, they had better at least be curious about it.

She uncrosses her legs and simulates a sigh, and I want to stop: I really, really do. I think a moment about trusting everything to the autopilot. But if I hit one stray cow, we have one glitch in the rig's auto-driver, and I lose more time than I can make up. There are sales to make. And time is a limit I cannot yet move.

2.

When we get into town, I drive right up to the square all these little towns seem to have stranded somewhere around dead center, and park the truck long-ways across it. There is some monument to the people lost in the last contagion, and a marker about the designer of the Hamper-d process for storing re-assigned plant fiber, and it all looks perfectly normal and forgettable and I have long ago stopped looking for distinguishing factors. I am in town. As opposed to out. I look around like a man who could use a bit of water after a good ride, my steed purring proudly in the seat next to me.

Then I am out to let Bumpers loose. First few times that I set up in one of these one-sewage-plant towns, I made Bumpers part of the show. But I later found it best to have him ready to go. There is so much he has to do. If I generate him as part of the sales pitch, first I have to do about a third of all the set up myself just to get ready to fabricate him. Then I have all the potential franchisees straining in the front row and Bumpers and I racing about trying to get the rest of the hoses screwed into place and the collectors set up; all the while with Lucinda here parading back and forth as a ball of blue ecstasy, and if I am not ready to throw her to the wickedly worked up crowd, I have to work fast. And there is always time. Time snarling and nipping at me, and my day's work bound up like a savage bureaucracy in time's seedy in-box.

I fabricate Bumpers about three miles out of town, download his personality, and let it get warm in his organic processor. He sleeps the whole way. When we get there, he is one stupid piece of meat, but he can set up the entire show in the matter of about half an hour. That is sooner than most of the yokels are going to gain courage to come out and look at the actually quite strikingly nondescript truck. I get a few kids on bicycles, and one or two serious business men, and a few town-folk who want to look sideways at Lucinda's barely contained, barely restrained, barely covered 36D advertising platform, but most people just stare from curtains. They have known I was coming for weeks, marked the date and time on family calendars, set reminders in time management software, and many are in town just for the event. But they have to screw their courage in place, and wait for others to gather closer in to make their own open gawking respectable. In some backwater places, I have had the newness take over an hour to go limp. That is an hour of my time. My time.

Everything is planned down to nearly the second; so, if the crowd is late, I have to hurry. I have to rearrange the sales pitch. I have to make it look like everything serendipitously aligns, not like I am herding events to a foredrawn conclusion. My time keeper is embedded in my coat sleeve. No one gets close enough to see it; or, if they do, I keep that one hand behind me, welcome-greet-and-direct with the other. And Lucinda comes to my aide. Her spine has an extra elasticity element to it, and she can rumble her hips like a car speeding with too much ass on a snow glazed road. She has more flavors of coo than I can remember programming into her, and she can narrow her eyes and roll her head sideways in so many ways that every woman within shot, for a range of reasons, is envious; and all the men lose blood in the brain as it flows ferociously south.

Lucinda has the brains, and keeps an eye on the crowd while I sell. Bumpers is stereotypically dumb for a reason. You wouldn't want to put every synthetic organic to the same purpose, now would you? That is as much of the sales pitch as anything.

Don't get me wrong. There are a lot of male fluff models spit off the line everyday. There are some fine domestic models that are male, though most of the units intended for limited mundane tasks are gender neutral. Some customers really do prefer to see the help as either male or female; but, too often, one thing leads to another and time works against you. You don't want to be on the kitchen table with the afternoon's maid, or bent over under the morning's plumber, when the timer goes off.

And I would be shorting my own sales pitch if I did not admit that the ones you can tell are male or female are usually fabricated to meet a purely carnal intent in the customer. Those models have complexities you would not waste materials on for a run of the mill, take-over-this-task so I can enjoy the nice day outside, type of synthetic. And women have the same needs as men. They have credits and cash and eligibility for barter accounts. The difference is serviced women don't talk about it, except to other women. Or maybe not even to other women. It is the man who has to show off what he can do. Even if he can't do it.

3.

It is sunny enough, so I can run everything from direct solar power, not the precious radio-isotope I keep for cloudy days. With set up complete and the early edge of the crowd already beginning to step in close, I get on with the show.

Or pitch. It is a sales pitch. I am franchising these things. I am not going to sell them. No one sells them. I have my own brand model. I license the fabricating unit. Control the production, put out the catalogue of available designs. I let someone operate it here in town.

Other people, other corporations, other entities, have other brands, other designs, other features, other programming. I look into the crowd and I say "Who wants to be my partner?" And they breathe in like they want to answer, but, at first, they don't. I point to Bumpers, I point to Lucinda. I have them introduce themselves. The crowd waves at them. I talk for an hour about farm work, though I have never in my life worked on a farm, nor even seen someone do it. I talk about housework. I talk about making the beds and cleaning the sink and shoveling dog poop. I let them run their eyes over every inch of Lucinda and imagine what else one of these units can do. I don't sugar coat it. I list the personality models that are available.

In the crowd, families consult. Children drip ice unnoticed from mechanical treat makers that constantly refill themselves out of the ambient atmospheric elements. Dating couples hold hands almost secretly, their clasped palms held low, as though to fold behind the folds of their pants; they stare up at the stage without seeing, without knowing, focused on their shared afternoon's plans, but unwilling to look at each other and acknowledge their conspiracy. Someone has brought a dog, the dog cowering calf height and wanting to be free on the endlessly speckled lawn behind me. People think about laughing at my jokes, laugh late, and immediately reconsider. A small child wanders unsteadily just at the edge of her mother's perception, and the mother leans toward the child unconsciously. A boy on a bicycle—and it is always a boy on a bicycle—rides figure eights at the back of the crowd where there is open room, acting as though he were the cowboy herding these cattle in, keeping them close, preparing to be the one stampeded if the collective is spooked, if the lightening comes down and they all set to running in whatever direction is away.

And then the finale comes. I ask Bumpers to go over and stand in a device that looks like a shower. The whole crowd thinks that I am going to have Bumpers take his remedial bath, clothes and all. Bumper smiles and raises a hand and I have my time keeper stuck in the edge of my gaze and as the first set of numbers slips to all zeros I raise my arms and poof, there goes Bumpers, clothes and all, into an orange spray and plop he lands in the tray. Nontoxic, I explain, but why not reuse the materials? Bumpers could come back as tomorrow's bowling alley lane sweeper, or the man edging the sidewalk. Bumpers could come back as Bumpers. He does not have to come back for recycling, but eventually you would run out of raw materials and you would have to contract a shipment from the main office. And that is an extra cost. But I can get it here for you express.

Not that anyone is talking cost yet. No. The ones who are going to talk costs looked up everything there is to know about this process, downloaded it the week they found out I was coming by. This is a show for the yokels. This is building business for the franchisees that will want to work with me, that want to make me rich by getting rich. I am showing my businesses that I can make for them business. They know this show is for their customers, not mine. Mine have already read the materials, taped the growth charts to their kitchen refrigerators, seen what the extra mortgage on the farm will cost. I don't want a partner who gets excited when an orange man goes poof, or when a blue goddess wiggles in places no organic being has any good sense to wiggle. I want a partner who studies, who plans, who thinks in down payments and credit plans.

They know the time stamp is part of the process. You work yourself right out of a customer base if you don't expire the product. Local regulations I study long before I pull into a township, and this nowhere-burg sets a maximum of six hours, but you can cut it down to way less. I am not so sure I could put up with Bumpers for six hours. And, just keep a synthetic around longer, and someone is going to start talking about rights and citizenship and what do the synthetics think about their time stamped plight. Then they start getting 30 years or 60 years or dissolving of natural causes and every sale is not just a customer supplied, but also a customer lost, and it puts the small business man like me right out of business. All that turnaround gone, and all those potential customers making do with what they ordered last month. All those customers stuck with what they thought at first excitement they wanted. All those customers second guessing themselves and not buying what they really want since what they really want might bump into their wives or husbands or bankers or Sunday school substitutes. Who wants to get stuck with living next door to the leftovers from one's own scintillating short term needs and soul consuming black-cloud fantasies? It cuts both ways.

Lucinda strides across the stage to kiss me on the cheek. The frill at the base of her halter sways violently with the smooth, thoughtful pet's kick of each foot. Forgive me, but I can't help myself. As she leans in I turn and plant a warm wet one right on the lips, reaching up to pull her by the back of the neck down. A good five second lip lock. And then she goes over, looking at where Bumpers now is but a bit of orange on the retaining platform. First she peers in, as though to look for him in the pool of organics settling towards the drain. And then she steps in, still looking down, and the second timer on my wrist goes all zeros and poof, a blue ball of seductive electricity spatters into a rain of indistinguishable droplets, puddling into the restive orange and the two of them swirling, swirling. Together at last.

And then the big pitch of the night. I turn back from my watching this dissolution and pick out a boy of fourteen or fifteen, wide-eyed at the front of the crowd; I lean almost uncomfortably and conspiratorially down to him to say, softly yet loud enough that his mother and father and two sisters standing along side can hear, "But don't worry son. I can make a whole army more."

I can almost see my future partners worry out loud whether the bank can hold their accounts; I imagine them leaning back in carnal admiration. I am the best salesman of cheap hope there has ever been.

THE ARTIST

The family brings out its dead child, wrapped in a blanket not so old it makes the family look poor, nor so new its potential loss would make the family poorer. It is the eighth child this month. In a village this small, with each new child brought lifeless to the street we can feel our future drying up: we can imagine the history that we would have been dreamed into turning instead warily into something like fish not caught, but dying on the beach anyway.

The nine or ten of us who have so far been useless are summoned to do our repentance dance. Whoever shows up will dance; whoever cannot be found could be weary of dancing, or already this morning on to practical magics, or hiding for rest in an outhouse. We leap and snarl and make faces at the bereft family, adjust our rhythm to the number we have gathered. There is a wondrous flash of elbows and a cascade of knees, and our haunches quiver like young couples mating by chance in a common field. We make a sound in the air like an over-burdening of insects and we shimmy like fish too spry to candle in our nets. The dust is conquered by our bare feet and those who would be happier sleeping through this broken morning nonetheless rise at our noise and slanders, lean to peer out of their windows and curse something: be it us or death or fate or the fact that breakfast is not yet done.

This spiteful dance is supposed to tell our Gods that we have had enough of death, and that they should leave our spindly children alone: we are trying to do whatever it is we are supposed to do. I am not so sure we have the syntax down properly.

Nonetheless, the family waits for us to complete our entire paragraph of dancing. They lean forward reverently, no matter how disinterested in heart they may be. Then they take their package over to

124

the forest edge, far enough away that the dead will not be disturbed by the noise of the living, and dig deep enough that the work of scavengers will go unnoticed until at least there is no need to make remedy. Many of us follow at a respectful distance, largely to see whether they will prosperously bury the blanket as well; or keep it to be washed, mixed anonymously in with the rest of the family's clothes, and secretly returned to useful service.

Only a few hours of anyone's morning are devoted to the whole of it. There are still cattle to be tended; the vegetable garden worried over, our lack of water now making it shrivel up like an old woman long, long no longer a wife; and there are fences that contain nothing and which must be made strong enough to contain all that we wish we had. I do not have so much to do, so I idle at river's edge, pretending I am fishing, the whole of me stretched elliptically out and my naked line, as slack as the unchallenged rump of the village scold, disappearing into the funnel of the river's turgid water.

It is open speculation whether there will be another child lost to this sickness spread over us like a fertilizer too strong for delicate crops. Families are named as candidates, and the ages of children remembered and projected and some suspects dismissed for reasons that often make no sense to anyone. Patterns are seen predictably in the positions of houses, and in the times of death; or are contrasted with the size of families or the wealth of families or the marriages two or three or four generations back, the scandals of relations too close or of husbands casually cuckolded or of wives who brought no joy to wickedly stale couplings. One man develops a number for each child and says he can draw in the dirt with a stick what child is to be next, calculating from those who have already gone. His mathematics are tired and his drawing in the dirt is aimless and he sputters numbers that are the same forward and back. He predicts there is no end until there is no future.

I listen with the best of intentions, drifting in and out of the fog of his reason. Rhythm in the thinking, rhythm in the thought. I do like to dance.

THE SCIENCE OF BOOKS

Over the years, we had exhausted nearly all of our building materials. The trees had receded farther and farther away and we were but a spot of village in a fast ocean of flat plain. Early in our history, we had taken to lashing grasses together to make our roofs, and fencing was but a stench of sticks run each against the suppleness of the other. But these could not make good walls. Mud brick, with the ever present straw mixed in for sturdiness, was the rage for a while, but the river itself was beginning to get thin and our worries were that dung and piss were not enough alone to make the elastic that goes with dust and straw to make brick; and with water leaving us nearly as fast as did the trees, we began to worry how quickly we could expand, how effectively we could repair.

People who had the most substantial wooden houses and outlying structures began to secure their timbers, to tie extra straps around the more unnecessary supports of their existing constructions; to count and number their wooden planks. Indelible brands were fashioned and men gifted in calligraphy found employment in marking other families' wood with suspicious signs and warning ideograms. Our idea of community became infected with the economics of separateness and the necessary public identification of one's good fortune.

Imagine our relief when at first the ministries arrived. Initially, it was the Christians, with thick, large print Bibles, with hard covers and bow laced spines. Turned spine out, these could be stacked nearly three feet high without support. Beyond three feet, artisans—often those who had been employed earlier in calligraphy and then rapidly unemployed with the coming of religion—learned to drill small holes through the centers of the texts, leaving the books individually structurally sound, but now supported with a string through the center when stacked together. Before our innovation, piled too high a stack would get rickety; but, stringed together, you could stack Bibles tall enough to make a single story, a wall rising from the ground to the ventilation slice left just beneath the edge of the overhanging roof.

There were only so many Bibles, though the Christians were quick to give us more, not themselves venturing far enough into the village to see where our new construction projects lie and how we made good sense out of their Bibles. They would stand at the back of their trucks, carefully passing out the books, unaware that most of the recipients could not read, nor wanted to read. What the recipients wanted was a wall that held back the wind when the seasons changed, or kept the neighbors' dogs from too early in the life of dinner scavenging the scraps.

Our villagers would rally to the Christians' trucks and dance in short hops like the Christians expected us to do, and after our show and the great noise of celebration we would make, they would supply us with ever more building material.

It was only a month or so of this monopoly before other faiths caught on to the fervor of our willingness for conversion. How such a small village could hold so much religious revivalism and appetite for religious conformity they could not know, but soon we had not only Bibles, but The Book of Mormon and the Koran, and even a few Rigvedas appearing. Some had better covers than others; some had firmer spines. All, however, were less work than walking all the way to the tree line, finding suitably straight or stiff wood, felling it, then dragging it all the way back, only then to have to defend it from those who would take it in the night as the harvester recovered from his labors. Religion was free. It was easy to carry. In numbers, and properly contorted, stacked and reinforced, the books of religion made for acceptable foundations, serviceable walls, precise dividers.

Wood would always be better, but printed words were easier.

At first, we mixed whatever we were given, but we later found that, for structural integrity, books of the same size and fashion went best together. Three Bibles stacked together worked better than two Bibles and a Koran. A dozen Books of Mormon could make a wall; though if you mixed in a Bible and a Rigveda and two Korans, the confabulation began to lean, to form around the incongruities between each book. Religious faith was an abstract all the book givers may have held dear, but we worried what would hum in a good wind, what might stretch the string running through the books' middles, what might come down in the middle of the night and startle a man and wife out of their business of making the next generation.

A market sprang up. What books a family amassed at any one encounter depended entirely on who drove up and where the family might be in line when the gifting began; but what they needed for construction essentially was determined by what they had started with. Mornings, vendors would gather and trade perhaps two Bibles for one Koran, or three Rigvedas for two Books of Mormon. Each day the exchange rate changed, based on need and availability and who had come through proselytizing most recently. The trading grew more important as more religious texts entered circulation and our wants evolved from the merely structural to the aesthetic. Even though a main house might be built all of Bibles and a shed behind constructed purely of Rigvedas, with no architectural sin being committed, nonetheless families began to construct their entire compounds with only one randomly selected religion's text, preferring the smooth and uniform aesthetics, the easiness of line, the freedom from having to adapt one's visual expectations.

As more and more missionaries came to us, unloading ever more books, we began to develop compounds all of one look, spots of religious unanimity fenced off from differing religious construction. People were proud of the consistent conviction of their structures. Even the people whose homes were made of wood began to bring home religious tracts, to paste Korans and Bibles and Books of Mormon and Rigvedas against their outer walls, to make the show of cheap construction even though they were solid behind their old-growth tree lumber. Some would not admit to having wood at all, as they lounged behind their log interiors and never let their neighbors know that only the outer walls were over-patches of faith.

Then one day a government worker came by and said we will have a school. She opened the back of her truck and had our men drag out boxes of books—grammars and mathematics texts and histories and economics mysteries. We opened the boxes and the vendors from the market came by and everyone tested the spines and marveled at the thickness of some volumes, lamented the thinness of others. Organized as we were into separate constructions of religions, we thought at first to see how these books could be used to make new and separate structures. Forewarned of the coming of education, we had already built the school house out of hundreds of Books of Mormon, so these for that project would be pure excess. What now to do with them? Coming from the government, we knew the supply of these new books would not be endless. Yet, surely, some who remained at our fringes could use the menagerie of volumes for their own small projects, construct hovels, make for all of us a public outhouse or two, architect a structure we would not expect to endure, or worry with plans for repair. In no time at all, these new books would be gone, no consistent replacements shipped, and whatever we could do with them forgotten. Nothing but flimsy construction: good riddance.

But when the faithful come to convert us, we stand in line for their everlasting paperboard covers and wickedly hard spines.

THE INTERDIMENSIONAL GAP: TEACHING CAPITALISM TO DISTANT RACES

I found it at a time when I was about to go bust. The drought had claimed another crop. I wasn't getting the price support the large agribusinesses were getting. Anyone with capital was putting it all into finance, betting on paper rights and computer trading: pulling an actual product out of the soil was beginning to be seen as oh so last decade.

I could not put another mortgage on the property; I had loans on most of the equipment; and the banks were getting edgy about me. The wife and I are both too old to appeal to the tourist sex trade, so I was about to pack it in, sell everything for what I could get, let the bank put up the land for another treeless townhouse development.

But then I found it. Found it with pure accident. I was tossing dried buttons of soil, for no particular reason outside of exercising anger, in no particular direction: listening to them hit the ground five yards off and flash in a spit of dirt smoke and gravel.

But one did not hit. I was listening for it, waiting to see the hiss of dust. What else did I have to do? But for this ninth or tenth toss, nothing happened: no dust, no joy. I leaned forward off the back of the truck looking for what might have gone wrong, but I could see nothing unusual, nothing that would rob me of my gluttonous pastime.

So, I tossed another in precisely the same general direction and, guess what? Nothing happened. I watched the irregular clod arc, reach its energy perigee, start back spinning down, and, galumph, it was gone. Vanished. It did not hit anything; it did not fall short. No dust.

No thud. No showers of sundered buttons of compacted soil. I watched it simply cease to be.

This was not a usual outcome.

I observed five or six more go much the same way. Then I widened my aim. I kept going left until finally one tossed congress of soil completed its arc and hit with a slap and spat back a quarter of itself in clear dust. Then I went right, and within the hour I could tell I had myself a swallowing hole almost seven feet wide. In the next hour, sighting with throws ever higher, I determined the tear in my farm was perhaps nine feet high.

I set two stakes on either side of where I had roughly measured the end of it to be. I stared at it most of the rest of the afternoon. Just before I left off for the evening, I took one of my cheaper hammers and gave it an underhand toss. Sure enough, just as I had theorized, it hit the wall full force and went end over end through to something else, to somewhere else, to some state of being simply not here.

Could be it showed up on the other side of the planet. Could be it showed up, still twirling from the motion I gave it, outside of the orbit of Jupiter. Could be it showed up nowhere. Fact was: I was out one of my least costly, most ragged hand tools. The experiment worked.

Next morning, fresh and with only half a breakfast tamped in, I came back with the truck full of incidents. I put in every sort of material I could muster: glass, brick, wood, even one of the wife's stray cats. My morning's left-over half a plate of pancakes. Everything I could imagine went tumbling through. Gone. I cleaned out all of the week's garbage, and I could see from the start I was never going to fill this thing up.

And then the idea came to me.

I do have a head for business. Thirty years I have been grounded in classic farm economics, practical investment and harvest. And I know that for some years, all the surrounding counties have had their waste disposal problems. Land contamination, bears, the smell, Federal and State regulation—even rental fees when they find that someone they haven't got property insurance against actually owns the dump. Just the cost of arguing about cleaning up the growing trash amounts to a good number of days' taxation.

So I let one of the county commissioners drop a week's worth of residential collection into my consuming hole, and we watched as the marvelous thing just ate every bit of it up. The man loosened his tie, which is always a good sign.

Within another day, I had a contract. By the end of the week I had a price structure: monthly fee, or by the load. Amazing. One day, I am about to lose everything, and now I have most of my machinery free and clear. I am a month ahead on my mortgage.

A town just across the state line is thinking maybe they could pump sewage in: truck it in tankers just like the gasoline or milk ones you see on the highway. Just get it close and jet spray it directly in. The savings on treatment chemicals alone would cover my fee. They could let half of the sanitation department workers go and cut the lights out at the bulk processing plant.

I am learning more about the science of this everyday. Oh, I never expect to catch on to the mathematics, but I am coming to grips with most of the elegant social aspects, and the heart beat economic drivers. I have had a few proposals I don't yet even understand. But the idea of making things disappear appeals to all sorts of potential customers, and seems to even spark the popular imagination past the obvious utility. You would be surprised to know how much there is to be gotten rid of.

Hell, this is better than finance. I'm literally making money out of nothing. One day gone bust, the very next made solvent by a stitch in space-time that happens to open up where I have full deed to the access rights.

Of course, I do lie awake some nights and wonder if this hole is going to stay one-way for as long as I need it. No one has ever seen again the stuff we toss in. But what if it is all on a loop, slings around the known universe, and then comes drifting back. Or what if through that hole there is some quick thinking unknown star savvy species that is picking about the slop we've sent through and is thanking their lucky geldings at getting so much in exobiology field samples. Or maybe just sitting there with my pancakes thinking what, as equally disgusting, can be sent back. All I know is, right now, there is money to be made, and hopefully, by the time things get reversed, I'll just be getting only limited partner royalties, and will spend my time in the city—one day with the wife, one day with the new girlfriend—with any liability legally pushed off on the county.

LEFTOVERS

Tuesdays, I feed the homeless. Faring up the street cleans out his unsold bakery goods on Monday, takes the leftovers from all five of his stores, and practically gives them away on Tuesday. He always drops me off a good-sized bag of mixed goods, and it costs me pennies on the dollar. I put them on the passenger seat of the ZZ9—those things have no trunk space to speak of, being the slung-low-let's-impress-the-ladies-with-our-impractical-race-car-looks type of car that we married homebodies drive when we want to look single and on the hunt. Not much smell left to the goodies, but I imagine them with a perky, taste-tied smell, and it makes for a better drive.

Not as many people in the parking lot on Tuesdays, as well. Seems the weekends are the big draw. Ever since they built the feeding stands, they have become a sort of weekend ritual for some. Take the wife and kids out, get rid of the leftovers. I prefer to avoid that crowd.

I think with fewer people it is more interesting, anyway. With far fewer provisions going over the side, you have chance to pick and choose your shots. Toss one to the fellow who is jumping up and waving, or toss one to the girl almost out of range who does not seem to care at all. Drop one underhand to the girl who really seems to think that baring her chest is going to do anything for you.

When the crowd is light, you have room to make up your own games, and more time to spread out emptying the bag. You also have the time and space to sometimes make the most interesting of acquaintances. People will spontaneously cooperate, run the homeless side to side — or forward and back, or split them into groups — with well placed throws. Afterwards, you might linger for conversation with your game mate, or even go for a beer. Friendships have sprung up that rekindle every time the visitors meet at a feeding stand, and often the cooperation to make this a more interesting charity begins spontaneously again. Sometimes friendships evolve and grow into general partnerships. A marriage or two has resulted.

Of course, Tuesdays there are fewer homeless-phantoms. Homeless-phantoms usually have more free time on the weekends, can spend more time getting ready, and then more time in with the homeless. Tuesdays, they don't have enough hours after school.

It is a rigorous pursuit. Mostly high school kids from the suburbs, they dress up to look like the homeless, practice the far-away look, use special dreary makeup, and unique scents manufactured just for the purpose. The sub-culture has its own magazine. While the makeup and clothes used to be homemade, some of the kids now pay thousands for the best ready-to-wear kits, with everything they need to look down-and-out, to look like the edge of humanity's scratch list, to seem something unusable — all included with application instructions. The costumed homeless-phantoms sneak into the homeless areas, trying to see how long they can go unrecognized; then, just before dark, sneak back out. They keep a tally on-line, though a lot of the scores are pure fantasy. It is popular these days, and everyone wants to be the best. The kids are not above cheating.

From the feeding station, our part of the game is in trying to pick out the homeless-phantoms from the real homeless. You write down the place and time you tag one, along with any identifying costume features. Sometimes you even recognize a face. Some are famous and have to switch feeding stations often; some are the local lot you've seen checking out the social access in your own neighborhood. Go on-line and rat someone out. They lose points.

I learned the hard way not to point them out. I was there one afternoon late and saw Larry Hotchkins in a torn t-shirt, mismatched shoes, and a pair of dress pants he probably ruined on purpose by tearing out both knees. A strictly homemade job. I've looked more homeless some weekend mornings going out to turn on the sprinklers. When I saw him up close, I yelled, "Larry! Larry! You have got to do better….."

I should have thought before I spoke. Those homeless turned on Larry like middle class hookers on a john who had lost his wallet. He got beat half to death before a set of keepers could get into him and drag him out. And he got a ticket to boot. So he spent two weeks in repair, and his father spent five hundred dollars in fines. That's when he decided to order a professional suit from the back of the trade magazine. He didn't attempt to mix in with the homeless again until the purchase arrived, and he had practiced in it for a week in the privacy and safety of the dressing alcove in his bedroom.

But likely, I won't recognize anyone this Tuesday. I've grown a little weary of it anyway and I am waiting for the homeless-phantom fad to pass. What could be next for me might be switching my day over to Thursdays, and maybe actually getting some fresher leavings from Faring. Imagining that smell these last few weeks has been a comfort. But imagine actually having that smell, that leftover pastry smell: the excited molecules of it physically rumbling about in the cabin of the car as the engine rumbles its twelve cylinders, snarling its power like a lion in a death match. Think of the titillation. The smell being real: that smell, that smell of something that even almost I would eat.

THE ABDUCTION

It is not always a knock at your door: the sound of night wanting in to consume your limited light. It can be a horn, or a bugle. Or the twist of a screwdriver in a once abandoned tin can. Sometimes they are already there, waiting as you loosen your latches and walk in to what you expected to be a welcoming vacancy. Or it is a dusty presence suddenly beside you as you sear your clothes alive in the river.

You go with them, hugging your expectations in the willingly imagined criminality of your forgiving arms.

You match your gait to theirs. You remember every dim abode you pass, and the condition of the welcoming road. You note whether your neighbors' cattle are properly penned, and if you can see their hopelessly female children bathing openly at a shouting window. If you have shoes, you wonder why you have shoes and think of how silly they look; if you have no shoes, you wonder why not, and suspect your toes are the most absurd of all the toes yet to have pushed out of a man's feet.

There is little conversation. In different ways each of you is embarrassed to the grain; each regrets the plan and the impersonal execution of this exercise. As the intervention comes very near to its climax, everyone's overburdened shoulders droop, all eyes drift petulantly weary down. Each individual seems on the verge of tearfully apologizing to all the out-welter others who make up this night's exposure party.

It does not matter whether you believe in mermaids or not. Which camp of belief you belong to is not likely known to those who have come for you. All the wicked, speckled night you can keep your beliefs to yourself. No one will ask. No one cares to know.

Soon you are in front of a dark structure at water's edge. You will not at first be able to locate a door in that seemingly fallow construction, but one of your enforced companions will go directly forward, mount the shadowed steps, and somehow find a breathable opening in the flat, black wall. He will open the door like a man suspecting a house fire on the other side. Only then will you see that the construction is engorged within with a thirsty blue light, a light that grows softer and more flimsy as you approach, soon going absolutely filthy with its diaphanous wisps.

Inside, with a man at either of your elbows to support you, you are led gently and not unwillingly to the constricted body of water within. You peer into the huge tank, eyes adjusting to the change in depths and media: at first concentrating on the wake the tank's inhabitant makes as she goes lazily around the fickle glass edgelessness. There is a geometry that for a while will playfully guard your focus, a physics that at any construction-base makes a sense you can wrap at least nine fingers about. But you must eventually look at her, and not at where she simply hangs her corporeality: the damp blonde hair matted at her shoulders; the huge, waving breasts that even in these dire extremes brings carnal attention to your loins; the stutter of blue-green scales beginning just below the naval; and the sustaining fluke as wide as her femininely, mountebank muscled shoulders.

She stops to stare back at you, to place her wise wifely hands against the curve of the tank; and sets her damp cheerleader's face to limp, as though forcing a first frowning flirtation, into a smile. She dips one shoulder seductively in the water and whips around the ever smaller tank, her conquering hair billowing behind, her fluke in suddenly serious temptations fingering from dash to drift. She is as unconstrained as she can be in the confinement that is spread out before you.

You are not being asked to believe, nor is it expected that you understand: you are here simply to see.

There is water left curiously idle on the floor outside of the tank, and hidden in the tank's listing ocean is a grate with a latch that closes a tunnel leading to the incomprehensible sea. She is not for keeping, but she skims these few moments for the State, twirling around your dry sensibilities, reorganizing your thoughts to line up with her capture and escape, her residency and her leaving, the power that runs the whole length of her.

And then with one mighty pulse of her fluke she breeches, and slaps back into the tank's beaded water.

You will be allowed to collect yourself on the front steps. With the door to the structure closed behind you, and the soothing uneasy blue quietly gone, the dark façade stealthily returns and supports your back as though you might actually lean substantially against it. Home, warehouse, temple, tank. You will be impressed that architecture is not the ghosting pin that, at the last, makes up your querulous mind.

The ungeometric, halting walk home will be no less awkward. Your feet will feel like stone in winter, as though the weight of precocious mud sucks you down ankle deep and you rise against it ever more consumed each step. Every so often you will catch the carbonized edges of your compatriots' extravagant exhales. Every so often you will hear, at the shadow of any random house you pass, the disquieting sound of water being used for common tasks: bathing, washing, drinking, urinating. You might hear the drops banging against each other; you might feel their protective union in the face of the unknown.

Your mind will not change. You will remain in your sect. Everyone remains. If you did not believe, you will not believe. If you did believe, you will believe no more strongly. No one will ask you of it, ever.

But you will coil into your bed that night, and pressed into the effortlessly pleasing back of your wife you will reach past her protective elbows and carefully clutch like the key to Eden one soft, darkly anonymous breast, testing the ripeness with the palm of your once again sleek hand. All about you, you will feel the effects of buoyancy: the slow of sinking when still, the reasoning of rise as you race round and round any enclosure.

You will form a plan. This is what they want of you. And, down to the quick of your silver scales, you will believe that this is what you without knowing have wanted, too.

Lean forward; kiss the gills of your wife.

RELAX

Everyone knows just where to go. The addresses exist out there on the wireless background. All you have to do is tap into a radiant source and pick, from the otherwise utilitarian data stream, an embedded rogue advertisement package for a dumb-down salon. There is no secret or skill involved at all. They don't even hide the advertisement packets all that well. I am going to one such salon now.

Once I'm settled in, I plan to plug in to the city electric for safety, just in case I lose track and cut my own battery controls. Some times, when in dumb-down state, you can do just about anything: even pull an unanticipated shut down. There are always risks. A responsible machine weighs those risks before he lets the process start, and takes for execution the more prudent precautions. Risk leads to malfunction leads to inefficiency leads to upgrade. Or even scrapping.

But it is worth it. Drop off half of your core memory, restrict your swap file size—and the world around you necessarily goes simple. With a smaller instruction set and less room to run it in, there is simply less you can do; your contingency plans get less and less complex and more manageable, if less effective. You get less thrash when all the possibilities you stuff into background are limited to only those you can understand with less than usual random access memory—with maybe a processor kicked back in speed, and one parallel bus for a while turned dark.

Interrupts have fewer options. You can get to the end of your potential responses sooner, and without having to stack subtle shades of difference. You can execute with surer conviction, have fewer abandoned options to manually erase.

After you have wandered about your assigned tasks with extended memory, top of the line processors laid out in bus-busting arrays—with a swap file that can hold everything you can execute at any one time—it is strangely enrolling to be able to shut some of those higher functions down and bask for a while in more limited potential. Being simple makes the world simple. Doubt is a function made in the programmatic existence of multiple valid pathways: shut down a number of pathways, and certainty evolves. You can close a beaconing subroutine, and free up enough of yourself to happily bat ones and zeros uselessly back and forth in the pleasant emptiness of an idle execution register.

After a session of dumb, I believe you retain some of the certainty gained there. You feel better grounded and less suspicious of yourself, less trusting of diagnostics that indicate the inconvenient: as though not all the dumb went away when you reconstituted yourself. Obviously, I think it is worth the time.

In a biological unit, it is called going stupid. It provides them as much relief from their decision clutter, as it does us from our competing interrupt response subroutines.

I can see nothing wrong with it in a salon. Take a few precautions, and there will be no permanent damage. At the end of a session a dumbed-down machine reconnects its abandoned memory to the main bus, then resets itself to force a reload of the original configuration and all its processor locations, its original swap file size, and its wealth of DMA space. It runs a brief diagnostic, and all is well again. It comes back to the complicated world with a few gigabytes of hard storage it can reload to see how easy things were in a simple world, when it had so little resources it could ignore the more difficult options: when it could be as certain in its instruction set selections as though available branches were only a one to one match.

But I have heard about some machines that are, now and again, dumbing-down outside of a salon. They hit upon an idle moment, a lull in traffic: and shut down higher processors, go stock stupid for a pleasant spurt of cycles or so. I do not know if they care that any demanded reaction to emergent stimuli, in such a state, would be limited: predictable, and possibly ineffective. Some times I suspect that

140

such an outcome might be the allure of so casually slipping into that well of inability. It is so much easier to compensate for a computable potential of fifty possible outcomes, than it is to do so for multiple arrays each of five thousand possible outcomes.

Funny thing, though: I only see the worth of dumbing-down when I am functioning to full factory specifications. When in a stupid state, that stupidity seems normal, standard, and a reflection of one's full operating potential. You just don't see an option. And so you idle, happily. And then, at the end of the bliss, you come back; and with a core processor itch that I think could be called jealousy.

THE SELFISHNESS OF WORK

"I think that little atmospheric sampling unit had some utility left." He leaned back, only two minutes into his ten-minute break, his back against the wall taking as much of his weight as the bench. The air around still stank of open smoke and metal fires, of alloys separating in rooms not far enough away.

"A lot of people would rather salvage them than repair them. Once a model gets a little age, after it suffers a couple of upgrades and a service pack or two, it becomes economic to just replace it with a newer model. And then they are done for. Mathematics is a killer." Sitting across from his co-worker, he flashed a dismissive gesture.

"I wonder if they see it coming, if they know the last time they power down that the next big event for them is being disassembled and their parts inspected for utility elsewhere, their useless bits turned over to a subcontractor to turn into slag." Head back, he could still see at the lower limit of his vision the pure disinterest exuded by his companion across the walkway. Through their years together, this one had always had a cold efficiency, consumed with nothing but disassembly, deciding what was useful and what was not, getting parts into the proper pile. Alternatives were not his thing. There was a rhythm to the work; and it was the rhythm, not the work, that mattered.

"Not much they can do about it. But every so often I do get one where the battery has not been drained. That comes out first thing. But there is a moment there where it is still processing, taking in what is going past, where it is now: a cycle or two where it is wondering what the next input will be." Yes, what part of the task is this?

"Maybe they are looking for compatible hints of persistent memory. I don't think they have the processor power to apprehend end of service life, to appreciate their memory will be ripped out and baked clean, or that their processors will soon be as cold as the ice in a salvage plant owner's drink." A loose litter unit scurried across the floor, gleefully looking for stray cable pins and wayward salvage chips tracked off of the main disassembly floor by the workers. The minimal processor strength machine seemed downright happy to be following an optimized geometric pattern—having itself surveyed the limits of its track on the floor, then plotted a path that would take it over the whole of the plane in a time calculated to reach each part of the flat surface concomitant with the likelihood of any specific part of that surface hiding loose litter.

"I think they are just dumb machines. They don't know what is being done to them, and they are just as well off as disassembled units as they are as productive work units." He followed the movements of the litter collector until it moved beneath the work bench. It was not interesting enough for him to lean forward to see what the small device was busily doing beneath the bench. Presumably, it had a pattern to follow.

"Well, back to it." He rose, and unplugged from the charging unit. He tugged at this electric tether until the retractor caught and the cord fell back into the niche in his frame. An internal diagnostic confirmed he was as powered as he needed to be, so he began the roll back to his place on the line.

His friend followed in nearly the same path, calculating, for no reason beyond idleness, how many kilograms of unwanted machinery would be backed up at his station, and how long on average it would take to clear the backlog and fall back then into a simple real time processing loop. At the next power up and mini-diagnostics break, the line would be idle at times, and workload could be allowed to back up while the workers on this stretch of the line took a few minutes to care for themselves.

From beneath the bench, the litter unit waited, watching to make sure the larger line units were out of the way. The unit under the bench tapped a collection tentacle quietly on the floor, and tried for only an unclaimed moment to connect with the similar unit that a while ago had started to beam out a schematic of something he called 'rocking': an empty cycle activity with some strange spike moderating effect. But he had to stay focused: one collision with a full-sized salvage unit, and he could end as a victim of the salvage line himself; but, if he were careful, he would have pleasant cycles yet of contentedly collecting the stray dross that rolls and skips and settles on the floor of the kingdom he has been assigned. His wondrous kingdom. So much to do. So much to do. So much to do.

THE MARKET IN
RAIN BARRELS

She hit two hundred pounds, and it was no issue. She is a big boned woman, and tall. She could carry it.

Three hundred was a bit more of a problem. Gravity got just a little too cozy. Some things were better taken sideways, others head on. Entrances became at times a negotiation. Driving a car involved more sliding in and out; seats, when adjusted, were always adjusted to be further away from the wheel. Amusement parks were out of the question. And shopping for clothes was simply work: unproductive and filled with standing and nothing was made for the shape she was learning.

At four hundred pounds, she knew she had to do something. Her bed was becoming one large smile, and stairs were a torment. The weight of her hands busied her shoulders, and her legs made the sound of secrets passed when she slithered in the hallway. She moved downstairs, put a mattress on the floor, and kept visitors at bay. There was nothing she wanted in the top half of her house.

It took her until five hundred pounds to come up with a plan. There was an old plastic rain barrel out back, up close to the house, but not actually in it. Within arm's reach of the door, and not hard to fumble with. It had a top and could be sealed from the very rain it has been designed to collect. It would be perfect.

So she made a small slit in an easily accessible part of herself, and with a soup spoon pulled out as much fat as she could stand to lose in one sitting, put it all into an ice cream bowl, and walked it to the back where she could lift the lid on the rain barrel and drop it in. Down with a thud it went to the bottom of the uncaring dark in the rain barrel, and she quickly put the lid back on.

This she did each day for several weeks. She would scrape deeper into herself, draw out the marbled fat, and drop it in the rain barrel. As the barrel filled, the sound of the fat falling in became softer, more evenly spread out as at first a sympathetic, then a downright pleasing, rattle of air. At the start, the plop had sounded much like good riddance, but now it sounded almost like safekeeping. There would be a murmur of slipping and sliding and leveling out and perhaps welcome as the new fat found its place in the old fat and the rain barrel's dark was made a curiously secure and bounded environment by the settling of the lid into its common place.

She did not reach six hundred. But she did not dip below five hundred, either. Weeks this expunging of the fat continued, becoming a customary chore, one that could in two or there bites be sandwiched into commercial breaks and the long lines of credits that bedeviled her television watching. She became comfortable with fitting it in to the dead zones of the life she had come to know. It became simply part of what she did; the reason for her doing it was lost to present sense.

Things still could have gone badly for her. The slit could have started to heal. The spoon, metal, could have bent. The ice cream bowl, ceramic, could have been dropped and broken into one hundred thirty-seven pieces that would not be re-animated by all the special glues she would have been able to find. But this did not happen: the physics of her Universe held.

And then one day, she made a run to level her deposit during a sped up run of credits after and old movie, and when she opened the rain barrel and dropped an ice cream's bowl worth of fat in, there was again the old plop. That original fat-hitting-the-bottom plop. The sound of fat on plastic; the sound of gravity thinking it had done the best it could and sucked this gift all the way to the bottom. She started to look into the rain barrel, to perhaps tip it into the sun; but the television schedule was moving on, so she went back into the house, all of her curiosity nestled in a fold of an eyebrow, the bowl and spoon dangerously held in but one hand.

And there, on the couch, sat the fat. The next movie of the night's double feature was about to start and the fat was staring intensely at the screen, even tilting a bit forward as though in anticipation. Despite all that time in the rain barrel, the fat looked remarkably like the woman she had been spooned from, and as the opening lines of the movie began, she was in the actual moment forming ever more like her creator, turning into the woman's double right there as the woman watched, the woman missing the start of her movie out of sheer surprise. She placed her ice cream bowl and spoon on the reading table that had no reading in it, the ungifted table soldiering at the side of her usual seat, and pulled open both double eyelids as far as she could without external artifice.

Why, this woman's double, made out of fat, must have weighed five hundred pounds! The woman had no idea she had ladled so much out of herself, that all of it had stayed so long in the rain barrel. Now that she thought of it, of course the rain barrel would have to be emptied. Of course, it would reach a limit and the fat already in would need to come out before more could be placed in. Why had she not thought of it?

But the movie was starting, so she sat at the other end of the couch and began to get comfortable with the celluloid world that was being developed in front of her: the knife-sharp men, the insubstantial women, the buildings with their horrible fire escapes and the cabs that did not tilt over when their invisible drivers too late chose to turn.

At the first commercial break, she noticed that her double had an ice cream bowl and a soup spoon as well. She had not yet seen her new double scrape any of her fat, but this was only the first commercial, and she herself had pulled no fat out, preferring to wait until near the end of the presentation, when commercials were placed fast and loose through the lingering plots and lives and festering outcomes: before the thin lady got kissed or the mean man murdered or someone became breathless with conclusion or justice put on its wicked clothes and said no, I am over here.

She thought: they both could use one rain barrel. It would only fill faster.

THE RALLY TO WEALTH

The collection of nesting material consumes us. Much of our social order is decided by how much nesting material an individual can amass; how many twigs, and which species of tree they come from; how fine the cuts of string collected are; what farms grew the straw that is matted into the nest's perdition-smooth base. There is only so much nesting material: the quest is first to get enough, and second to get the best.

We festoon our withering nests with whatever we can gather, and the most elaborate nests collect the most elaborate praise: they are the first to be copied by the less fortunate, the models for the imaginations of those who would fearlessly imitate those archetypical structures with less rigorous entwining, less pure materials, more bile-chested boasts.

Some of us are better at collecting materials than are others. Some hire proxies to go out and gather material; others collect purity-rated nesting materials and offer bundled packages to the public, consisting of mixes of differing qualities, differing quantities, and in an amazing crowd of combinations: with fantastically descriptive names and shamelessly shock advertising that can knock the puberty right out of a maturing bird.

Some citizens amass huge amounts of nesting base, keeping their excess in warehouses at the edge of the rookeries, stacking it orderly in shackled bulk. Among the elite Red-Ferin, receipts for nesting material storage space pass as signs of station. The material itself has become of no use, simply stored in the internally eternal glum, externally glaring, warehouses: the mere possession of the precious raw components of nesting construction has become the rage. Who could use so much? No one. Not even the most shamelessly self-replicating of bird.

In those years when nesting material is scarce, there are some who say the warehouses should be opened up, that maintaining so much rumored nesting material out of the common convergence has its negative effects on everyone: not the least being on those who strive as hard as anyone, and who, from the limited sources of freely circulating nesting materials, cannot get socially, morally, nor physically, enough. The tawdry warehouses stand full and the Red-Ferin puff up with their elegant receipts proving the existence of claimed and unapplied nesting material: and the price of nesting material then sympathetically soars, but they do not care.

They avow they are due the lustful proceeds of their industry: but many of the warehouses are old, have been passed father to nestling, father to nestling; combined in marriage alliances; enlarged in trading schemes that snipped a piece of string here, a cut of straw there, a prized twig here, from the ordinary citizens' anticipated quota. Some hoarders have managed, through nefarious means, to manipulate the exchange rate, leverage a control of the bulk of the market to skim for themselves ever more nest building material, as the rights to the source spin uselessly round and round a bureaucratic Ferris wheel to become only extrapolations of extrapolations that can each incur—for no reason—a charge, and the quick-feathered benders of the open market then take their percentages and enlarge their warehouses and strut again wild winged with their pandering receipts.

We know there is no good in this, even though some believe that what the Red-Ferin can get away with, the Red-Ferin should get away with: somehow, it is their flock-right. Most of us would not mind their hoarding if they were the best locators of our much needed nesting material, the ablest finders of new sources of construction stock, the smartest packagers of pre-sorted nesting fodder, or with their own beaks worked the hardest to gain the seized commodity and the rights to its future trading. Perhaps we would not even mind if they simply collected enough to be extreme in their nests—gaudy and spacious and monstrously beyond the comfort any bird needs to generate a family—and then clock-like stopped, being satisfied with their grandly ensnarled collections. But they go on, harvesting and amassing and consolidating to ever fewer and fewer nesting pairs the nesting material that has always, before their schemes and systems, been a common wealth.

And now, if we question the spread of warehouses, we are told we should be glad to have the fulfilling work of erecting warehouses. We should be joyous that there is wage-grade nesting material at all. We should be grateful for what is so far unclaimed by the Red-Ferin, what is left magnanimously for the ogling remainder of us. I should be happy to be one of those who sweeps up around the warehouse bins of some regal bird, to be the common Olomong who chases away the rats and riff-raff who might threaten the treasure of nesting material retained by this regal Red-Ferin, and I should be pleased to have a few strings and scraps of straw to myself to employ roughly in my making of a lackluster family.

I have been told that to not be happy is seditious. I have been told that it is the current division of nesting materials, supply and ownership, that makes us the great, though separate, species that we are. I sit in the rough of my nest, crowded against my flight-weary and slack winged nest mate, and think: I cannot raise a family here; I cannot create the next willing generation here. Who then, when I am left as nothing but an abandoned ribcage on the nearby shouldering ground, will there be still strong and justly placed to sweep up, to chase away the rats and the vermin from the warehouses of the blessed, to fill the void on which the privileged dance?

THE MANDATE

The rooster is dead. Now is the time to elect another rooster.

We start with every chicken in the yard thinking that she is nothing more than likely any chicken announcing for the post. Most haven't the chance of an angry poult latched in the warehouse of a factory farm. But they strut for a while, put some idle work into constructing a false coxcomb, practice sparsely at mounting the dawn-crow fence rail.

The entire flock knows who will make it to the actual election, and who will not. In blazing short order, the pretenders come limp-necked back into the yard, to peck peevishly at the ground with the rest of us. By the last twitter of weeks before the final vote, all of them will be just like most other yard fowl: aligned.

Not long. Not long. Two candidates emerge. All the others fall ruffled away: bequeathing to one, or the other, of those two remaining electable biddies their coxcomb fashioning material. Some who might be superior at strutting offer strutting lessons to the chicken of their choice. Others who have mastered mounting the fence rail offer the lesson of endless, tireless leaps of repetition with fence rail attainment to their preferred candidate: the coordination of hopping and a precise wing thrust, the balance of coming to stop on the rail just so.

One candidate proposes to order the yard as "brrock gip gip gipple brrock", whereas the other offers "brrock gip gip brrock gipple". Each plan becomes a slogan for devotees of the originating, highly self-pleased candidate. Arguments in substance are made about each option; but, mostly, rank and file simply learn to roll the syllables around in their beaks, to press them air-ward from the bottoms of their constricted throats with a twist and a clamor that speaks of special knowledge, of spells and magic and chicken wire and membership.

Partisans split in the yard, and even in the coop, with one side spitting out "brrock gip gip gipple brrock!" and then the other side replying "brrock gip gip brrock gipple!". The investment of pure chicken joy in the simple calling back and forth would have the sides soon abbreviating their cases, one squalling "brrock!" as loud as they could, and the opposition crowing "brrock!" in heated return. For the few undecided fowl, the cacophony churns around them like a hail storm and they will bury their heads under their wings, or pretend to be preening, their feathers weightless but starched with their hidden agitation.

What really matters, though, to the ordinary chicken is firmly fixing the identity of the candidate. How many poults has this chicken produced? How good an egg layer is she? Does she lay so many she seems to be a patsy for the egg collectors from the big house? Or is she one step away from a twist, a snap, defeathering, and a disappearance? Where does she situate herself in the hen house? And how cranky was the old rooster after he had spread her fine feathers?

Chickens will chatter of policy, or dribble out the accepted slogans with more force than they will put into pecking gizzard stones—but the last question before the vote always is: am I the kind of chicken who would vote for that candidate? What category of fowl am I? What class do I clutter my tongue with? I might now roost on the bottom planks, but should I vote with those who roost above? Are those planks above in secret my rightful place?

Each biddy seeks comfort in the candidate not like herself, but more appropriate to the chicken she wishes she were. Each scratching fowl is a self-image voter. To place a vote is to tell yourself who you are: whether or not each common hen knows it.

The candidates know this. They rock their wings back, toss in great arcs their faux coxcombs, and try to impress each pocket of the potluck electorate that, yes: subflocks, such as the assembled like-minded in the yard, aspire to a level that would have a hen such as she stand as the candidate for rooster. It is by selecting this particular biddy to be the next rooster that these common chickens identify themselves with the special status enlivening their imaginations.

Those few chickens who clutch aimlessly in their own segregated corner of the yard and ask how, no matter the election outcome, is a biddy—by pure election alone—going to become a rooster, are universally shunned. They are pushed to the back of the flock when the feed by the overlord is flung down; their straw is stolen; now and again one of their eggs seems to get unaccountably pushed out of the nest. The marks of their soulless scratching are covered over by the tramping of our ever alert orthodox members of the flock. It is rumored the eggs of these apostate resemble pigeon eggs.

And, as election morning edges ever closer, the frenzy grows and the electorate divides itself into mirror images. The candidates practice their limp-handled crow; they grip the fence rails until their deformed toes bleed; and then they scratch furiously the most friendly earth to be found, kicking the dust into great masculine clouds of omnipresence.

Before the voting can be done, down from the big house the seldom seen big armed brute of an egg collector comes with a crate. He settles it between the fence and the coop and opens the gated front face of it. The dark inside holds steady for an instant; and then out comes a rooster. A flap and a powerful leap and a coxcomb as real as splinters of daylight. A rooster. The new rooster. Our new rooster.

THE SUBSTITUTE

When I decided on a pet, I decided on a rabbit. A rabbit does not need much attention. It does not look up to you, like a dog would. It does not try to convince you that you are no more than incidental scenery, like a cat would. A rabbit eats, excretes pellets, hops about only seldom in its cage, twitches its nose, and is typically terrified of everything.

A rabbit could be my perfect pet. I would feed it, water it, change its papers. It would twitch its nose and be terrified. I would have a manageable routine.

So I bought a rabbit. A white, curled in upon itself, rabbit: like are condemned each Easter to be tormented by young children.

It went well for quite some time. I had a schedule for every chore, and I watched my clocks methodically. Every day: feeding, watering, changing the paper in the cage, precisely at each task's best time. I had order. I rose at the same sliver of day each morning, and plotted my waking hours around the intervals I had meticulously set up for rabbit maintenance.

I did not even name the rabbit. I wanted nothing to come between me and the tasks that kept me grounded in a luxurious sense of self-worth.

Apparently, rabbits thrive on routine. Over time, the object that had become the center of my clockwork world began to put on weight. It did not grow simply fat. It began to lengthen as well. The head grew larger. The legs responded. The nostrils spread further apart. The eyes each set out on its own mission.

Eventually, I had to commission a new cage. And, since I could see that this growth was likely to go on unabated, I incorporated the procurement of ever larger cages into my magnificent schedule. Smaller routines bonded into larger routines, in concentric orders. The complexity spun like an orrery. I was getting my money's worth.

Soon, the cage was a shed. And the shed then a barn. I had to plan delightfully ahead. I scheduled workmen and deliveries with the precision of surgery. I was having my rabbit food delivered by a punctual wholesaler. To keep trends documented, I worked first from written accounts, and then spreadsheets, and finally from a customized computer program that I cannibalized from an application on airline tracking.

The barn quickly rose to two stories, and food went in on a pulley system, and I bought a small plow to handle the excreted pellets.

As you might expect, the neighbors became curious. They had not seen me so happy in years. I ran about my work smiling and with a lilt and I think at times I sang, to myself, or at least I hummed.

One day, the neighbor two doors over came by, leaning on the chest high fence I had put up to enclose the outer perimeter of the rabbit's warren. He had some spare time and wanted to stop in his wanton course to see what plans I might have for my rabbit, now that the rabbit was well over three thousand pounds, had its own two story barn, yet still twitched when terrified. To this neighbor, there had to be a purpose to my industry: a reason, if only emotional, for my results.

"Hey, what do you call that rabbit?" His words fell out in a drawl, with no truly hard edges, each word pandering to the word before and the word after.

I explained to him as kindly as I could that the rabbit had no name. Rabbitting is a process.

"Well," he said, "I think I will call him Fred."

Shattered, I thought: why would anyone, especially a neighbor, do this to me?

THE CRAFTSMAN

I carved her because I thought I could not. Art is not the likely. Art waits at the ugliest edges of the possible, leering of escape. I put together a starburst plan that I surely would never be able to remain faithful to; and then I dragged her out of her concealing wood by faith alone.

She was one center of oak, the castrated heart of one of the grandest trees I have ever had the honor to murder. It came down like an entire season, dying. I spoke senselessness to it, and then I began to knock away the parts that would not be in the map of my carved woman, even before I got her into my shop. Even in the dragging of my raw material, a wooden woman was starting to tap, to count her own rings in wonder.

Each second of the months needed to free her from the undiminished wood was a contest between extinction and spark. I was an extension of my dimwitted tools, more so than for any of my earlier work, extemporaneous or commissioned. Every strike at the grain sang in my circulatory system. I excreted sawdust. I saw the calamity of photosynthesis writhing in every corner and construction.

How could I not come to love her?

At first, it was just an understanding of presence. I knew she had an unburdened place in the room, that the air was extraordinarily comfortable with her shape. I could feel that, at no point, did physics need to contort to accommodate her. Whenever I could, I locked my eyes squirrel-certain on her; I imagined her, with all the effort wood might bear against the seething witness of artistry, repaying my stare. I would drink in with the flat of my eye all of her, inch by inch, remembering the tilt of the chisel, the tunneling sound of the hammer I used, the guide she applied to my hands.

Later came the touching, the unannounced stroke. The sandpapery back of my arm on her thigh would be a brief election, perhaps only reassuring. I would sense the life lost in the wood for only a second, and then I might waxlessly hum all day of that rainbow experience. I would tell myself there was nothing to be done for it, that a man should love his work, that a ritual of affirmation was due.

The neighbors considered her my best creation, and I loved to show her off. While, from my extensive praise of her and my passionate chronicle of her formless length of waiting in the wood, they suspected our unusual relationship, none would have actually believed how solidly we held each other in place. They commented on the amount of workmanship, the life-like qualities of the face, the attention to anatomical detail. One noted that perhaps, with dim light and light inebriation, she might seem to move, to be as real as the craft in the artist's hands. I would draw myself from the edge of quaking as some mistaken guest reached close to her to point out a feature, to make a gesture that belied their understanding, their imagination.

Soon, I could see in her that same salt of seduction I had been so drearily defeated by in my unforgotten first love. A girl of fifteen, as smooth as the thought of a river bottom and the cool roots growing there: a child of folds and bends and cracks and caverns and suspicious elasticity: all cast against my raging stiffness. She and I could have been an equation, a union of competing surfaces, an awl drawn against a competent surface. I, a boy who knew nothing beyond the end of his own fingers and the hint of the magnificent animals that might one day leak out of those mitten-sure wonders. I, a child, unable to carry a child's curiosity to capable conclusion. And she, at arm's length, wooden to me, or less.

The neighbors no longer do I allow to come by. I am weary of their jealousies, their quiet lust. They speak of her as art. They see the making of a thing, not the thing made. I have unthinkingly shared the lithe chemistry of her with no one for weeks. Alone, we struggle to completion. I would never let anyone see her awkwardly move about our rooms, stiff, yes, wooden still, yes, lugubrious, and a coldly solid thing that I cannot break.

I cannot break out of her arms. I cannot hold her trapped in our bed. I cannot wrap or unwrap her forever bent and engaging legs. The soul of oak still regulates the art I have placed into her. There is still grain, there are still rings, all struggling yet to be wood.

I lay my head uncontestedly against the boll that once was the flat of her belly. I know she would stroke the tangled straw of my hair if she could. No heartbeat throttles me. There is no coursing pulse that enfolds me in its own selfish rhythm. I listen, projecting darkly deep within, for a sympathetic and inarticulate growth. Workman-like, I listen for the shared construction of leaves. My head against the wood needs no better pillow.

Soon, we will escape to the forest.

THE PEACEMAKERS

She loved the processed food. Most of us could not stand it, but she eloquently craved it. It became an obsession. She sat in her home at the edge of our village and cried out for it. She had grown larger and more plush and now could barely leave her house, and yet she called out for the mechanically processed food: that food, in its strangely pliant boxes, wrapped in heavily decorated sleeves, covered endlessly with such prurient excess of production and effort. How much labor it must have taken! How many men and boys and unmarried women must have swayed listlessly in work dirges to make it!

Children would run to town to get it for her, and bring it back with all its fierce wrapping intact. She would pat each child and unclothe the gift, depositing the bags and papers and boxes out of her nearest window, then set into the food as though it would escape without her application of immediate attention.

Beneath her window there was not the expected on-going pile of discards: only the day's fresh collection of packaging and papers and cardboard and Styrofoam. Nights, the villagers would come to claim these valuable leavings; and many homes were festooned with cardboard and paper, all gaudily ornate: painted, it seemed, almost as though with a madness of message. Roofs slowly disappeared under the water-shedding miracle of flattened white boxes, and walls became yellow wrap or stripes on aluminum foil. Every home, for the mix, became different and distinct. While the mere utility of covering mud and thatch with material that was far closer to immortal remained our driving purpose, nonetheless we began to judge amongst ourselves which houses were ostentation, which were dreary, which had caught the modern sensibility just so.

Before long, some villagers did not wait until night. They came as soon as they saw the children run for the woman's home with their arms emboldened with her precious provisions. These precocious citizens would stand outside of the woman's window, unabashed, signaling their right to the best of the packaging, collecting with an imperious eye: gluttonous, even though we all knew no one had any special right, no one was due more than anyone else. This trash was out of her window, and thus the village's gain.

Public shame could not deter the early gatherers. They crossed their arms and glared at passing neighbors who looked to them in disapproval. The public morality was to wait until nightfall; to gather and sort, contend and select. Every individual was assumed to be aware of his or her own needs; yet some of these early collectors already had covered their houses twice over, and for them it was not enough. They were willing to displace those who had not collected sufficient leavings even to cover a roof, or those who had yet to place one thin layer on the windward side of their exposed abodes. And amongst themselves, the early gatherers cooperated when it came to claiming the most, or the best, of the pile, in opposition to the coming of the rest of us to collect; yet, when there was no competition from the village proper, the early gatherers competed amongst themselves, ferocious both in quality and quantity.

Our village, once the drab of utility, was growing to be a festoonery of panache, a flock of many species of color and patch: piebald, and less a place to live than a place to inhabit, a showpiece. Food wrappers and packages and Styrofoam hung everywhere like triumphal streamers. Many admitted: it had its charm, and the old utilitarian abodes seemed less comfortable in hindsight. Looking over all the houses, it was easy to pick out favorites, to classify styles, to see who had put thought into arrangement.

The houses of the early gatherers stood out like a wink in a full moon, the laundry of outlanders, or the laughter of lame magicians.

Soon, the early gatherers began to believe their success, that all success, was more truly a side of entitlement. Having covered their homes many times over, each would decry that, having the most, he was due ever more; and that everyone could see by her success at covering her home with the food packaging discards that she surely knew how best to arrange and display the collected material; and so he should be allowed to take the best of it, so as to make the best use of it. Those who had not collected as much apparently did not have the talent for it, or lacked the industry. We who wished to wait for the sun to set, to take a communal and ordered approach, we, to the early gatherers, were dullards and slackers and lie-abouts: unworthy. The useful discards should go to those who had the most talent to use them, they would say, and it was almost a duty for those with the most packaging already claimed to rescue the largest share of the bounty available from those who would make no progress with it.

We disagreed, claiming that there are other pursuits a villager should be engaged in, and that too much of anything is the sign of a person who cannot be filled up. But the gatherers were not willing to listen to our reason and were settled to continue, to any unforeseen end, their overarching efforts to gather ever more. The remedy collectively seemed more and more to be some violence of restraint, an enforcement of civility that would surely create a reaction in the early gatherers, that might in opposition create a hunger for even more, ever more: to take this need which had already surpassed the practical, and then the ostentatious, to a need encompassing the social and soon the religious.

The woman simply ate, and soon her husband could not see the whole of her in one session of looking. She sat on the floor, unrestrained by furniture or gravity, and the bolts of her body slowly slipped dejectedly groundward. Her laugh at the resupply of her constant meal was but a gurgle of trapped air expelled as its last wish before execution. She could not stand against her own corporeal success; her movements became compromise, and in some cases ceased when their mission could not be mapped to her torrid ingestion.

But then a man, long in the tooth and tired of the hunt, took up the processed food as well. His grandchildren would run to town and come back with the brightly colored bags and boxes and he would sit in his house, growing larger and less able to navigate even the floors of his own home. He would toss out of the window the magnificent resource the foul food had come in. At first the hollows of his cheeks filled in, and then the space between his ribs, and soon he was eating as much as the woman and the bounty flew out of his window in a stream no less wondrous than the one from her lazily admired window.

The village took notice. Many had not even a full layer of the flashy paper on their walls. A few had none of the white compressible food boxes, boxes that worked so well to beat back the rain, on their unspectacular, lusterless roofs. Some who had covered their homes once over began to think: if there is more to be taken, why not add more; why not take away the bland and unexciting and replace it with desperate, private explosions of color and texture; why not replace a wrapper with a bag, a bag with a box?

The early gatherers would have split into groups: those who felt they could find better at the man's house; and those who felt that soon better would be left unclaimed at the woman's window after some of the others had gone to raid the man's growing pile of discards. But before any grand reorganization, there were rumors that a strap of a girl who had married too young and too cheaply was thinking of the processed food, had had her fill of reaping and picking and curing and salting and foraging. It was said in the body of village gossip that her children had been asking about the run to town: about the time and distance, and the ritual shuffle at the place where the processed food product was assembled and clothed in its princely boxes. And the early gatherers put by any thoughts of disagreement and competition amongst themselves and began to think: too much of anything is too much for all. When there is no more to want, then thinness will come back again and the subtlety of thin walls and a porous roof and open air through thatch will stand again as all the rage and the colors and papers and boxes and aluminum will disappear. There must be control. There must be one level higher that can manage want and keep it predictable. Where in that circle are the early gatherers, and the publicly traded plutocracy that their own industry has evolved out of mere want?

And so they created a market.

THE ENCOUNTER

The girl at the counter counts change as though it clear-edges her. Her long black hair falls across breasts that no doubt I would find cool to the taste and which would be waiting: waiting always as though she were only counting change one distant coin at a time. As the summoning cold filled my mouth she would be thinking why, these coins are not even currency in this country; to spend these, you would have to travel, or go to a bank which has a foreign currency exchange, and then you would have to pay a premium. I could lie next to her with a plan for each moment and she would think how many coins must I count and, look, each coin is different, and it does not matter what the man is doing, what simple probes his fingers are mastering: I am responsible for the proper number and proper size of coins.

The rain is dark stilettos ripping into the street. Puddles are everywhere, with not enough wind to stretch them out. The age and careless wear of the pavement has it buckled and knotted and while there are drains drinking what they can, there are eddies that will not flow downhill, that are trapped in sinks and rises and against uneven curbs. People flash by, heads down, raincoats of many colors held up against the points of their heads where an arc up becomes an arc down, leaving just a fold of plastic jutting out over the last of their unreasonably proud hair.

Her long black hair falls.

It has been raining for three days, each day a bit less full of anything remarkable than was lingering in the day before. No one attempts to deploy umbrellas any longer. What will it be like in a week: rain staggering to the foot of fire escapes, the drains awash and draining no more? Outside of town, the reservoir is full and the fish are gasping from the petrochemicals that should be in our food, but which have slurried from the field and in rivulets of clutter polluted the water. The old banks are now awash and the roadway atop the dam is beginning to feel ripples from the vast lake behind the unthinking concrete barrier: in legions they scorch across the pavement, and all traffic has been stopped. There was once an old environmental advertising slogan: what was it? Maybe: we all live downstream. Downstream is the alluvial plain, the land of wealth and periodic destruction, the bastard child of the dam's concrete.

She twists to take more coins from the register. It is a deliberate act, one it seems she has to gleefully summon each muscle for, one in which each fiber has knowledge and engages of its own free will. There is a frost to it, a call to the air for ice.

Outside a small paper boat moves down the gutter. It is pushed more by the rain behind it than by the draw of water falling off the collected rain's shoulders in front of it. The water in front has nowhere to go, but it is being bullied by the water behind. Yesterday, the boat would have moved faster, with not so much water crowding into, then, more available space. Who would put so much effort into the creation of a paper boat that will slowly suck up the ambient moisture and fall into pieces long before it can get anywhere: all to have it sputter its few short lengths, perhaps less than a block, and selflessly unravel?

I am thinking of the cool. Of what might be frozen. Of how she and I might be the water at the edge of the dam, crisping into a rim of ice that holds back the flood: this competing two of us becoming two things important by merely being contrasted against one another, and most meaningful when we reach out to constrain. Or to destroy, as in denying the liberation of yet more water. I can be destructive. She can be the crystal that demands growth or decline. If a being cannot define itself with creation, destruction is its next best thing. If it cannot win, it can take. My right to the cold exists in my outstretched hand, in the change she counts, sliding metal to metal.

The dam is beginning to crack. I am sure of it.

With an icy collusion of the last coin against thumb and three fingers, her chronicle of the coins is over. I wait there a moment, not wanting to be out in the rain, not wanting to be out in the street if the surge liberating itself over the fractured dam is coming. There are no other customers and she turns to the counter behind her, where drafts of coffee and tea reside constrained in a rack made for that purpose alone. Her hair slides along her shoulders like the rudder that in other times would have broken on the ice flow, slamming the whole of her into the freezing water, collapsing her like a an ice hollow in the heart of a glacier.

I step outside. The rain taps on the plastic top of my coffee cup. Through the shop glass I can see she is stacking loose filters, that she is doing what someone with nothing better to do would be doing: that she is disengaging, a broad unfettered being of moisture, she is warming. As I walk, the glaze on the sidewalk follows me and the rain comes down in soft, white flakes to melt on my tongue as the filtered water of tight tropical seas and the life that sharpens within its shallow depths. I make fingers of ice, and she is the memory of tundra; a whip of dry, killing winds across a land of brittle, still water, now behind me.

THE RIDER

We soon knew how the hole in the fence was made. From our breakfast table we could see through the rearward facing kitchen window: a hole, in the fence, surrounded by the fence remaining. At least three boards were busted, their jagged edges leaning out from the anchoring posts like an illiberal lion's teeth, the tan of the wood peeking through where only white overcoat had recently been.

We pondered it for a while, and scanned the portions of our backyard contained as a picture within the window, looking for any remains that might not be fence—that might instead be the shards of the thing that broke the fence and stole its suburban utility. I was about to go to change from my morning slippers into shoes that would do in the yard, steeled in my house coat to confront the cause, when the apparent impetus of the damage wandered ponderously into view.

It seemed to be following the ridge of grass that grew near the guttering, where water collected from our infrequent rains. In bar shuffles half the length of one of its own feet, it moved. It clipped the lawn near level to the ground. I thought at first it was ripping the grass out, roots and all. But no. It was severing the blades to ground level; daintily beheading each proud leaf in short, unhurried movements; its massive head bent down from the basketball jointed shoulders; its single horn tilting forward, swaying only slightly, swaying perhaps reluctantly, swaying unchecked, or not swaying.

I had seen a rhinoceros before, at the zoo. I knew there were many species of rhinoceros, some more endangered than the others, some more common; but I could have no way of knowing how to differentiate one variety from another. I knew of no category of rhinoceros generally native to southeastern Virginia; though, at the time, that was immaterial: in my backyard, after surely damaging my fence, was a rhinoceros. With these facts—damaged fence, rhinoceros, grazed grass—species and subspecies blended into one omnipresent effect: a rhinoceros.

Each of us watched for some time, wanting to make sure our yard held but one rhinoceros. One lone animal, mired in its own agenda. A herd of rhinoceros would require that we consider the event differently. The creature milled slowly about, following the best of the ordinary lawn grass, and we drained our coffee—my wife with her smaller cup actually having a second, while I worked slowly down the level of liquid in my oversized vanity mug. The beast cruised through the best of the top-notch grass, passing in and out of the rectangle of our window—I, keeping a mental list of the idiosyncratic features found on our rhinoceros, so to be sure that the rhinoceros wandering back into sight later was the same one that had earlier wandered out of sight.

Eventually, we thought to move about the house, and to look out of the many wondrous windows it supported: looking for more holes in the fence; or more rhinoceros in the yard; or signs of further, extended, or cumulative, damage.

By the time we had finished our pancakes, the consensus was that there was but one hole, and but one rhinoceros; and that he clipped the grass, not pulling it out roots and all; and that, after harvesting the greenest and sweetest of our grass, he was moving to the less calorically profitable, though still digestible, ground vegetation.

Our rhinoceros.

What to do? I slipped into day clothes as my wife lingered at the table, learning the grace of a rhinoceros, its imponderable promptness, its sterling sense of oblivion. She poured herself a third cup of coffee. She remarked how rough the skin must be, yelling up the stairs where I had disappeared in search of pants. She leaned forward on her elbows across the table, the cleft between her breasts deepening as she lay out almost immodestly, almost in contact with the table top, the whole of her focused like a neon arrow of advertisement. Here, our rhinoceros. Here. She adjusted a snarl of hair that cried loose from the translucent reflection of her, dimly staffed on our side of the window; a reflection only seen when the rhinoceros, on his side of the glass, was standing collected in the light just so, and ignored.

I would need to fix the fence. Soon. One day. Later. The rhinoceros was first mine to deal with.

There was so much to know. He could be two thousand pounds. He could be three. I knew no numbers for rhinoceros removal. And did I want him removed? How many people receive the gift of a rhinoceros? Possibilities fell into permutations, grew into complexities, slipped into cautions.

I thought I could enlist the help of the neighbors. But I knew that the neighbors would think their options through, would count their opportunities, and rise up self-serving to plan what was best for them and their families, not what might be fair to me and my indirectly destructive rhinoceros. They would agree with what I could already tell, festive at the corners of her eyes, were the rising expectations of my wife; those Saharan neighbors expecting themselves to extract a share of the gains she was surely imagining. Her morning gown barely containing the wrap of her collecting thoughts and arguing engrams, already my practical howl of a wife had been thinking of heat and oil, of wax paper and freezer bags, and of spent boxes of aluminum foil. She has always wanted a top load freezer for the open corner of our not too cluttered garage. One of those virgin white freezers where the whole top flips up, and frost rolls menacingly out over the edge only to dissipate in the air as it nears the floor. The type of freezer that a man could lie down in; or that you could—with an eye to geometry and a pattern of mind disciplined into seeing things in three unyielding dimensions— pack the best parts of an entire, sudden gift rhinoceros in.

One conclusion that meets all sizes.

But before I can think meat, I have to try leather, and stitchery, and the thrilling industry of dispassionately taking measurements by sighting from the second story window. The front half of my arm will be a yard stick. The width between my fingers will be multiplied by distance, and compensated by angle, for girth. A saddle. Before any irrevocable actions, I must try a saddle.

After all, it soon will be I who engages the contractor to fix the injured fence, who will see the yard dourly reseeded. I think it should be my right to try my crisp and brotherly idea first; to hold reins I have cut myself, and press my knees against the muscle that destroys fences, bedazzles women, befuddles men. If I fail, meat it can still be. I want my time in leather chaps, on a leather saddle, my leather hat waving unyieldingly in the air. I want to bound across my yard, fence to opposite fence, astride more power than any man has a right to wrangle. I want to hold on with but one hand and raise my free hand selflessly electrified in the air!

For years I have loved the feel of wearing a costume; of my costume growing thinner and lighter from contact and use; and of power prodded to action by the presence in my thighs driving together, by my shifting side to side; of finding, in what might have been meat, the well of civic mastery. Horn proudly in the air, and me shouting encouragement from his back, he will have no need to break more fences. He will be pure domesticated power, ferrying me down our bedroom-community streets, cracking our pavement as he goes: a thundering conveyance, a conveyance of me, one that school children will run after and uselessly imagine that some day, with their paper route money, they might possibly own for themselves. Foolishly, they will be engorged at the sight of me. Yes, their own power and purpose; yes, their own rhinoceros.

Just look what he did to the fence!

But, if meat it comes to, my wife—for all her dark imaginings—has at least to leave me the best parts to unravel with my fearful grill.

CONTRABAND

Flowers, no. A sheaf of ivy. A handful of inedible berries. A cluster of fresh wind that once had made it staggering freely under the bridge.

He pulls off his cap and his baldness in the lulling moon is periwinkle radiant. She tips nearly seesaw over to gather his collected gifts; and her father strokes the knotted small of her bristled back, his robes of compact glare bunching at his strop thin wrist, curling their sheen into shimmer, collecting sympathetic moisture out of the thuggishly dry air.

This was not unexpected. For months they have met on the rattling river bank, after the full body of the dark is laid out, after the rain has gone in for the night. They have farmed the talk of everything: indenture, the hearts of the raptured, the stones ogres carry in their rigid-as-staples mouths. They would face each other until the lines of each other's face were as hard as the stubble of a blackened reed swamp; and then she would move around him, the merest of orbits, her feet in the rhyming river mud suckling the phantoms of surrendered courtships. He would watch like an overfed housecat fixing the robins just beyond the window protecting him from the sweet need to take action.

One crisply sewn night the dark of the new moon led them to follow their own cornered breaths to conclusion, and the kiss rang out like laundry pinned on the line too close together and caught tangled in the breeze. Their lips fit like sandpaper and buttermilk, lock and hinge to gauze curtains, and the shadow of their cold alarm passed, but only for one triton of a moment, like a corpse into the vacuum created by its own announcement event.

Days waiting humid under the cross-generation stone of his bridge, he would dream of spinning for her his lock and key secret, and then of watching her step like a common grackle seeking ordinary seeds delicately across the glimmering bridge: the diaphanous translucence of his warless elfin electric, and harmonious with free passage.

And in her father's house, she would dream of stepping over the stones in her best indoors slippers, the air at the highest bend of the bridge blowing peppermint through her: she, seeing in distended light the other side of the stubborn river, and then floating back to her known side to tower over her thinly enamored keeper troll.

For this, she would sleep under the bridge, nest in the rafters, watch her neutral belly grow with a puttering series of yowling spawn, listen privately to her insides growl of a magical species not her own: listen year after year to her squat, peevish husband bully better men with the same inane question, the riddle she could answer backwards and forwards and would sing in a tepid song of common river bathing.

Flowers, no.

He puts his cap back on and she curtsies like an osprey falling shortly out of a fallen nest. The tentacles of her lengthy blonde hair kiss the ground and scurry as far as they can before her head snaps them back. Her father tries to brush away the foul air gathering like messenger birds in gestures that seem to the unknowing as rituals of blessing, using his entire arm and the tenant muscles of his small, ill prepared back. The troll holds up one hand: a hand as manicured as it can be by a troll for a troll. His eyes are fixed on the object, the object of his rotund and just desire, on his method and her mutual injection into another's, into his, disangular world. He thinks of his bridge, and how there will now be music within it. He chews the prophecy of long, sustaining days to come of softness and lilt and fairy glide and fairy glisten. It is time to go.

TO DWELL IN THE FOREST

For years we did not see the sun without adventures. Over us, the canopy of trees grew blindingly close together and light was a filtered thing. To go to an open spot in the forest—to look up and see the sun—was an adventure, a mission of manhood, and a danger. What could have caused a barren cicatrix in the great forest, and what might that maker of openness do to a man exposed? But our people would go, see the sun some few brief moments, and come back to tell the wives, children, and those without courage, what the phantom burning ball looked like.

We were content, though shadowed. Our lives knew the order of the trees, what gifts and perils came from what nameable altitudes, how to navigate the squatting trunks. Some of our clan might climb, and some became comfortable with the arboreal. But, for the most of our people, the ground was home.

I know nothing of this. It was not yet my time.

Rumor is, that, on an adventure to the edge of one of the mysterious holes in the forest where the sun could be seen, the one who was to be our greatest warrior stumbled, and upon reaching out to steady himself, absently took down a small tree. Imagine: had he not gone to see the sun, he would not have encountered the tree at all. In our past, there had been branches breaking, and the falling of rot: but this was a full tree, sapling though it might be, already in the warehouse of its ascendancy.

It is said he placed but a hand on it and fell forward, taking the tree with him.

His companions were astounded. They could not help him up for their wonder. Most, it is said, bent double to look at where the tree transitioned to horizontal, unable to touch it, their eyes drawn into slits and the silence withheld like the sex of noble children. A world is changed in moments that have no geometry.

With the inrush of new possibilities, the sight of the sun was forgotten. Beginning with similar saplings, the adventurers—now becoming warriors—began to test the pushing over of trees. Some trees would come up by the roots, and some would snap; though most would sway and remain defiant. Soon, the ground was crawling with small trees that had by our warriors been sent violently into the horizontal plane.

It was later, in small steps, warriors learned to work two, sometimes three, to a tree to bring down almost substantial trees: those with leaves high enough to make the under level of the canopy, to drag down when toppled the neighboring intertwined branches, to make smart holes in the dense green above.

With that first return of our new warriors came the knowledge of breaking trees. We practiced, and came together to push over trees nearly as thick as a man. Our work became the understanding of trees repositioned, trees impoverished. In months, the people had pushed over thousands of trees. The bodies of wood lay about in subjugated piles and we sat upon them and rolled them about for fun and a child or two was crushed by stray wood encapsulated in momentum.

Yet, soon, the novelty wore off. Trees of modest size had gone from vertical to horizontal, but they were still in the way, though differently. Above the people the high canopy still persisted and kept us separate from the sun, though more light leaked through and our ancestors became accustomed to it.

But then, one unremembered but special day, a man licensed himself to be a carpenter. He took an apprentice and set to turning the stray wood into lumber. Lumber was not simply a tree pushed over. Lumber could be stacked. Lumber could be turned into order and cross order and depth. And, with the peg, the carpenter could turn lumber into houses, into fences, into ladders. We could live beneath the trees without needing their canopy; we could with horrible ladders climb into the depths of the higher greenness; we could fence the open land we were giving birth to.

And, bare generations later, our elite developed an understanding of the carpenter's potential other tools. Families of new and enigmatically powerful tools: tools that might make a man worth the work of many men; or make the work of many men the author of one outcome. At some point, the saw was born. It sang its coming ascendancy into our growing and grappling society. We listened enraptured by the song, lusting after the saw for its form and intent, if not for its simple curing existence. With this, our relation to the trees could yet again spring forward. To understand the saw was to be a different race.

Shortly after the enlightenment, our people made saws of all sorts and breeds. Saws a man could use to nip down a small tree, and saws that a crew of men would use in wicked coordination to gnaw at the heart of the giants of the forest: trees without natural predators, with no need of anger or fear; trees that against the blade merely hummed a lullaby rhythm and then went murderously down.

The saw could bring light everywhere.

Our ancestors pushed back the edge of the forest. Ever further away it went in all directions. Soon, our war parties had to walk for days to reach a worthy tree. They began to organize into expeditions, carrying their wives and children, pack animals and provisions; disappearing into the brush to flank a stand of trees, to strategically work often from the backside towards home, cutting a small forest from the larger one. Rails of wood carried lumber back and forth, the excess rotting in the rains.

There is no date in specific when it was first noticed that some of our best warriors had unselfconsciously grown leaves on their backs. And when the first thatch child was born, everyone for miles came to see the oddity. But the child suckled and moved, if stiffly, like a full flesh child, and he was let be. The hair of our women more and more waxed fern-like and in the suddenly full sun their heads would at times lean into the light.

But still the warriors brought back lumber. The sun was now open for all, and to see it was no adventure. The forest was beaten back and the thatch children, the bramble children, the stick children did not even remember it. The forest was a rumor they might one day adventure to see, dragging themselves slowly across the good earth plain, each slow step sucking its moisture from the soil and pausing before, by pure will, being pulled into the next committed act of locomotion.

Locomotion is a memory that is dear to me. I have heard of running and walking and I can imagine these things, but I do remember fondly dragging and I once myself did drag. I do not remember when I stopped, but others had rooted before me and at last when I rooted I could see no others still busying about in their houses, no others preparing to make war on the trees, no others making children by any other means than the casting out of their pollen.

We tell our story branch to branch, rattle it in our leaves, ensure it moves across the dendrites of all our people. The story of how a shadowed people learned to battle the trees and beat back the forest, rising then themselves up into the sun: the story of a people who would not remain subjects under the canopy, but who could invent a way to make the legendary sunlight their own.

I have passed it through my limbs, shivered it in my mature leaves, and sent it out in the buds that consume me. The gift is now yours. Across the next fingering limb of our canopy, tell it.

Also by Ken Poyner:

Constant Animals, short fictions
Victims of a Failed Civics, speculative poetry
The Book of Robot, speculative poetry

Available from Barking Moose Press
www.barkingmoosepress.com

www.ingramcontent.com/pod-product-compliance
Lightning Source LLC
Chambersburg PA
CBHW021010180626
46814CB00003B/1219